Passport
Birth certificate
Jewish activities
Holiday Schedule
Clothing

Return mail/money
DOGS

An Owl Book
Henry Holt and Company
New York

Fight Club

a novel

by

Chuck
Palahniuk

Henry Holt and Company, Inc.
Publishers since 1866
115 West 18th Street
New York, New York 10011

Henry Holt® is a registered trademark of
Henry Holt and Company, Inc.

Published in Canada by Fitzhenry & Whiteside Ltd.,
195 Allstate Parkway, Markham, Ontario L3R 4T8.

Library of Congress Cataloging-in-Publication Data
Palahniuk, Chuck.
Fight Club: a novel by / Chuck Palahniuk.—
1st owl book ed.
p.   cm.
"An owl book."
1. Millennialism—United States—Fiction
2. Young men—United States—Fiction.
3. Apocalyptic fantasies.   I. Title
PS3566.A4554F54   1997   97-20023
813'.54—dc21   CIP

ISBN 0-8050-5437-5

Henry Holt books are available for special
promotions and premiums. For details
contact: Director, Special Markets.

First published in hardcover in 1996 by
W. W. Norton & Company, Inc.

First Owl Book Edition—1997

Designed by Antonia Krass

Printed in the United States of America
All first editions are printed on acid-free paper.∞

1   2   3   4   5   6   7   8   9   10

For Carol Meader,
who puts up with all my bad behavior.

Acknowledgments

I would like to thank the following people for their love and support despite, you know, all those terrible things that happen.

Ina Gebert
Geoff Pleat
Mike Keefe
Michael Vern Smith
Suzie Vitello
Tom Spanbauer
Gerald Howard
Edward Hibbert
Gordon Growden
Dennis Stovall
Linni Stovall
Ken Foster
Monica Drake
Fred Palahniuk

Fight
Club

I

TYLER GETS ME a job as a waiter, after that Tyler's pushing a gun in my mouth and saying, the first step to eternal life is you have to die. For a long time though, Tyler and I were best friends. People are always asking, did I know about Tyler Durden.

The barrel of the gun pressed against the back of my throat, Tyler says, "We really won't die."

With my tongue I can feel the silencer holes we drilled into the barrel of the gun. Most of the noise a gunshot makes is expanding gases, and there's the tiny sonic boom a bullet makes because it travels so fast. To make a silencer, you just drill holes in the barrel of the gun, a lot of holes. This lets the gas escape and slows the bullet to below the speed of sound.

You drill the holes wrong and the gun will blow off your hand.

"This isn't really death," Tyler says. "We'll be legend. We won't grow old."

I tongue the barrel into my cheek and say, Tyler, you're thinking of vampires.

The building we're standing on won't be here in ten minutes. You take a 98-percent concentration of fuming nitric acid and add the acid to three times that amount of sulfuric acid. Do this in an ice bath. Then add glycerin drop-by-drop with an eye dropper. You have nitroglycerin.

I know this because Tyler knows this.

Mix the nitro with sawdust, and you have a nice plastic explosive. A lot of folks mix their nitro with cotton and add Epsom salts as a sulfate. This works too. Some folks, they use paraffin mixed with nitro. Paraffin has never, ever worked for me.

So Tyler and I are on top of the Parker-Morris Building with the gun stuck in my mouth, and we hear glass breaking. Look over the edge. It's a cloudy day, even this high up. This is the world's tallest building, and this high up the wind is always cold. It's so quiet this high up, the feeling you get is that you're one of those space monkeys. You do the little job you're trained to do.

Pull a lever.

Push a button.

You don't understand any of it, and then you just die.

One hundred and ninety-one floors up, you look over the edge of the roof and the street below is mottled with a shag carpet of people, standing, looking up. The breaking glass is a window right below us. A window blows out the side of the building, and then comes a file cabinet big as a black refrigerator, right below us a six-drawer filing cabinet drops right out of the cliff face of the building, and drops turning slowly, and drops getting smaller, and drops disappearing into the packed crowd.

Somewhere in the one hundred and ninety-one floors under us, the space monkeys in the Mischief Committee of Project Mayhem are running wild, destroying every scrap of history.

That old saying, how you always kill the one you love, well, look, it works both ways.

With a gun stuck in your mouth and the barrel of the gun between your teeth, you can only talk in vowels.

We're down to our last ten minutes.

Another window blows out of the building, and glass sprays out, sparkling flock-of-pigeons style, and then a dark wooden desk pushed by the Mischief Committee emerges inch by inch from the side of the building until the desk tilts and slides and turns end-over-end into a magic flying thing lost in the crowd.

The Parker-Morris Building won't be here in nine minutes. You take enough blasting gelatin and wrap the foundation columns of anything, you can topple any building in the world. You have to tamp it good and tight with sandbags so the blast goes against the column and not out into the parking garage around the column.

This how-to stuff isn't in any history book.

The three ways to make napalm: One, you can mix equal parts of gasoline and frozen orange juice concentrate. Two, you can mix equal parts of gasoline and diet cola. Three, you can dissolve crumbled cat litter in gasoline until the mixture is thick.

Ask me how to make nerve gas. Oh, all those crazy car bombs.

Nine minutes.

The Parker-Morris Building will go over, all one hundred and ninety-one floors, slow as a tree falling in the forest. Timber. You can topple anything. It's weird to think the place where we're standing will only be a point in the sky.

Tyler and me at the edge of the roof, the gun in my mouth, I'm wondering how clean this gun is.

We just totally forget about Tyler's whole murder-suicide thing while we watch another file cabinet slip out the side of the building and the drawers roll open midair, reams of white paper caught in the updraft and carried off on the wind.

Eight minutes.

Then the smoke, smoke starts out of the broken windows. The demolition team will hit the primary charge in maybe eight minutes. The primary charge will blow the base charge, the foundation columns will crumble, and the photo series of the Parker-Morris Building will go into all the history books.

The five-picture time-lapse series. Here, the building's standing. Second picture, the building will be at an eighty-degree angle. Then a seventy-degree angle. The building's at a forty-five-degree angle in the fourth picture when the skeleton starts to give and the tower gets a slight arch to it. The last shot, the tower, all one hundred and ninety-one floors, will slam down on the national museum which is Tyler's real target.

"This is our world, now, our world," Tyler says, "and those ancient people are dead."

If I knew how this would all turn out, I'd be more than happy to be dead and in Heaven right now.

Seven minutes.

Up on top of the Parker-Morris Building with Tyler's gun in my mouth. While desks and filing cabinets and computers meteor down on the crowd around the building and smoke funnels up from the broken windows and three blocks down the street the demolition team watches the clock, I know all of this: the gun, the anarchy, the explosion is really about Marla Singer.

Six minutes.

We have sort of a triangle thing going here. I want Tyler. Tyler wants Marla. Marla wants me.

I don't want Marla, and Tyler doesn't want me around, not anymore. This isn't about *love* as in *caring*. This is about *property* as in *ownership*.

Without Marla, Tyler would have nothing.

Five minutes.

Maybe we would become a legend, maybe not. No, I say, but wait. Where would Jesus be if no one had written the gospels?

Four minutes.

I tongue the gun barrel into my cheek and say, you want to be a legend, Tyler, man, I'll make you a legend. I've been here from the beginning.

I remember everything.

Three minutes.

2

BOB'S BIG ARMS were closed around to hold me inside, and I was squeezed in the dark between Bob's new sweating tits that hang enormous, the way we think of God's as big. Going around the church basement full of men, each night we met: this is Art, this is Paul, this is Bob; Bob's big shoulders made me think of the horizon. Bob's thick blond hair was what you get when hair cream calls itself sculpting mousse, so thick and blond and the part is so straight.

His arms wrapped around me, Bob's hand palms my head against the new tits sprouted on his barrel chest.

"It will be alright," Bob says. "You cry now."

From my knees to my forehead, I feel chemical reactions within Bob burning food and oxygen.

"Maybe they got it all early enough," Bob says. "Maybe it's just seminoma. With seminoma, you have almost a hundred percent survival rate."

Bob's shoulders inhale themselves up in a long draw, then drop, drop, drop in jerking sobs. Draw themselves up. Drop, drop, drop.

I've been coming here every week for two years, and every week Bob wraps his arms around me, and I cry.

"You cry," Bob says and inhales and sob, sob, sobs. "Go on now and cry."

The big wet face settles down on top of my head, and I am lost inside. This is when I'd cry. Crying is right at hand in the smothering dark, closed inside someone else, when you see how everything you can ever accomplish will end up as trash.

Anything you're ever proud of will be thrown away.

And I'm lost inside.

This is as close as I've been to sleeping in almost a week.

This is how I met Marla Singer.

Bob cries because six months ago, his testicles were removed. Then hormone support therapy. Bob has tits because his testosterone ration is too high. Raise the testosterone level too much, your body ups the estrogen to seek a balance.

This is when I'd cry because right now, your life comes down to nothing, and not even nothing, oblivion.

Too much estrogen, and you get bitch tits.

It's easy to cry when you realize that everyone you love will reject you or die. On a long enough time line, the survival rate for everyone will drop to zero.

Bob loves me because he thinks my testicles were removed, too.

Around us in the Trinity Episcopal basement with the thrift store plaid sofas are maybe twenty men and only one woman, all of them clung together in pairs, most of them crying. Some pairs lean forward, heads pressed ear-to-ear, the way wrestlers stand, locked. The man with the only woman plants his elbows on her shoulders, one elbow on either side of her head, her head between his hands, and his face crying against her neck. The woman's face twists off to one side and her hand brings up a cigarette.

I peek out from under the armpit of Big Bob.

"All my life," Bob cries. "Why I do anything, I don't know."

The only woman here at Remaining Men Together, the testicular cancer support group, this woman smokes her cigarette under the burden of a stranger, and her eyes come together with mine.

Faker.

Faker.

Faker.

Short matte black hair, big eyes the way they are in Japanese animation, skim milk thin, buttermilk sallow in her dress with a wallpaper pattern of dark roses, this woman was also in my tuberculosis support group Friday night. She was in my melanoma round table Wednesday night. Monday night she was in my Firm Believers leukemia rap group. The part down the center of her hair is a crooked lightning bolt of white scalp.

When you look for these support groups, they all have vague upbeat names. My Thursday evening group for blood parasites, it's called Free and Clear.

The group I go to for brain parasites is called Above and Beyond.

And Sunday afternoon at Remaining Men Together in the basement of Trinity Episcopal, this woman is here, again.

Worse than that, I can't cry with her watching.

This should be my favorite part, being held and crying with Big Bob without hope. We all work so hard all the time. This is the only place I ever really relax and give up.

This is my vacation.

I went to my first support group two years ago, after I'd gone to my doctor about my insomnia, again.

Three weeks and I hadn't slept. Three weeks without sleep, and everything becomes an out-of-body experience. My doctor said, "Insomnia is just the symptom of something larger. Find out what's actually wrong. Listen to your body."

I just wanted to sleep. I wanted little blue Amytal Sodium capsules, 200-milligram-sized. I wanted red-and-blue Tuinal bullet capsules, lipstick-red Seconals.

My doctor told me to chew valerian root and get more exercise. Eventually I'd fall asleep.

The bruised, old fruit way my face had collapsed, you would've thought I was dead.

My doctor said, if I wanted to see real pain, I should swing by First Eucharist on a Tuesday night. See the brain parasites. See the degenerative bone diseases. The organic brain dysfunctions. See the cancer patients getting by.

So I went.

The first group I went to, there were introductions: this is Alice, this is Brenda, this is Dover. Everyone smiles with that invisible gun to their head.

I never give my real name at support groups

The little skeleton of a woman named Chloe with the seat of her pants hanging down sad and empty, Chloe tells me the worst thing about her brain parasites was no one would have sex with her. Here she was, so close to death that her life insurance policy had paid off with seventy-five thousand bucks, and all Chloe wanted was to get laid for the last time. Not intimacy, sex.

What does a guy say? What can you say, I mean.

All this dying had started with Chloe being a little tired, and now Chloe was too bored to go in for treatment. Pornographic movies, she had pornographic movies at home in her apartment.

During the French Revolution, Chloe told me, the women in

prison, the duchesses, baronesses, marquises, whatever, they would screw any man who'd climb on top. Chloe breathed against my neck. Climb on top. Pony up, did I know. Screwing passed the time.

La petite mort, the French called it.

Chloe had pornographic movies, if I was interested. Amyl nitrate. Lubricants.

Normal times, I'd be sporting an erection. Our Chloe, however, is a skeleton dipped in yellow wax.

Chloe looking the way she is, I am nothing. Not even nothing. Still, Chloe's shoulder pokes mine when we sit around a circle on the shag carpet. We close our eyes. This was Chloe's turn to lead us in guided meditation, and she talked us into the garden of serenity. Chloe talked us up the hill to the palace of seven doors. Inside the palace were the seven doors, the green door, the yellow door, the orange door, and Chloe talked us through opening each door, the blue door, the red door, the white door, and finding what was there.

Eyes closed, we imagined our pain as a ball of white healing light floating around our feet and rising to our knees, our waist, our chest. Our chakras opening. The heart chakra. The head chakra. Chloe talked us into caves where we met our power animal. Mine was a penguin.

Ice covered the floor of the cave, and the penguin said, slide. Without any effort, we slid through tunnels and galleries.

Then it was time to hug.

Open your eyes.

This was therapeutic physical contact, Chloe said. We should all choose a partner. Chloe threw herself around my head and cried. She had strapless underwear at home, and cried. Chloe had oils and hand-cuffs, and cried as I watched the second hand on my watch go around eleven times.

So I didn't cry at my first support group, two years ago. I didn't cry at my second or my third support group, either. I didn't cry at blood parasites or bowel cancers or organic brain dementia.

This is how it is with insomnia. Everything is so far away, a copy of a copy of a copy. The insomnia distance of everything, you can't touch anything and nothing can touch you.

Then there was Bob. The first time I went to testicular cancer, Bob the big moosie, the big cheesebread moved in on top of me in Remaining Men Together and started crying. The big moosie treed right across the room when it was hug time, his arms at his sides, his shoulders rounded. His big moosie chin on his chest, his eyes already shrink-wrapped in tears. Shuffling his feet, knees-together invisible steps, Bob slid across the basement floor to heave himself on me.

Bob pancaked down on me.

Bob's big arms wrapped around me.

Big Bob was a juicer, he said. All those salad days on Dianabol and then the racehorse steroid, Wistrol. His own gym, Big Bob owned a gym. He'd been married three times. He'd done product endorsements, and had I seen him on television, ever? The whole how-to program about expanding your chest was practically his invention.

Strangers with this kind of honesty make me go a big rubbery one, if you know what I mean.

Bob didn't know. Maybe only one of his huevos had ever descended, and he knew this was a risk factor. Bob told me about postoperative hormone therapy.

A lot of bodybuilders shooting too much testosterone would get what they called bitch tits.

I had to ask what Bob meant by huevos.

Huevos, Bob said. Gonads. Nuts. Jewels. Testes. Balls. In Mexico, where you buy your steroids, they call them "eggs."

Divorce, divorce, divorce, Bob said and showed me a wallet photo of himself huge and naked at first glance, in a posing strap at some contest. It's a stupid way to live, Bob said, but when you're pumped and shaved on stage, totally shredded with body fat down to around two percent and the diuretics leave you cold and hard as concrete to touch, you're blind from the lights, and deaf from the feedback rush of the sound system until the judge orders: "Extend your right quad, flex and hold."

"Extend your left arm, flex the bicep and hold."

This is better than real life.

Fast-forward, Bob said, to the cancer. Then he was bankrupt. He had two grown kids who wouldn't return his calls.

The cure for bitch tits was for the doctor to cut up under the pectorals and drain any fluid.

This was all I remember because then Bob was closing in around me with his arms, and his head was folding down to cover me. Then I was lost inside oblivion, dark and silent and complete, and when I finally stepped away from his soft chest, the front of Bob's shirt was a wet mask of how I looked crying.

That was two years ago, at my first night with Remaining Men Together.

At almost every meeting since then, Big Bob has made me cry.

I never went back to the doctor. I never chewed the valerian root.

This was freedom. Losing all hope was freedom. If I didn't say anything, people in a group assumed the worst. They cried harder. I cried harder. Look up into the stars and you're gone.

Walking home after a support group, I felt more alive than I'd ever felt. I wasn't host to cancer or blood parasites; I was the little warm center that the life of the world crowded around.

And I slept. Babies don't sleep this well.

Every evening, I died, and every evening, I was born.

Resurrected.

Until tonight, two years of success until tonight, because I can't cry with this woman watching me. Because I can't hit bottom, I can't be saved. My tongue thinks it has flocked wallpaper, I'm biting the inside of my mouth so much. I haven't slept in four days.

With her watching, I'm a liar. She's a fake. She's the liar. At the introductions, tonight, we introduced ourselves: I'm Bob, I'm Paul, I'm Terry, I'm David.

I never give my real name.

"This is cancer, right?" she said.

Then she said, "Well, hi, I'm Marla Singer."

Nobody ever told Marla what kind of cancer. Then we were all busy cradling our inner child.

The man still crying against her neck, Marla takes another drag on her cigarette.

I watch her from between Bob's shuddering tits.

To Marla I'm a fake. Since the second night I saw her, I can't sleep. Still, I was the first fake, unless, maybe all these people are faking with their lesions and their coughs and tumors, even Big Bob, the big moosie. The big cheesebread.

Would you just look at his sculpted hair.

Marla smokes and rolls her eyes now.

In this one moment, Marla's lie reflects my lie, and all I can see are lies. In the middle of all their truth. Everyone clinging and risking to share their worst fear, that their death is coming head-on and the barrel of a gun is pressed against the back of their throats. Well, Marla is smoking and rolling her eyes, and me, I'm buried under a sobbing carpet, and all of a sudden even death and dying rank right down there with plastic flowers on video as a non-event.

"Bob," I say, "you're crushing me." I try to whisper, then I don't. "Bob." I try to keep my voice down, then I'm yelling. "Bob, I have to go to the can."

A mirror hangs over the sink in the bathroom. If the pattern holds, I'll see Marla Singer at Above and Beyond, the parasitic brain dysfunction group. Marla will be there. Of course, Marla will be there, and what I'll do is sit next to her. And after the introductions and the guided meditation, the seven doors of the palace, the white healing ball of light, after we open our chakras, when it comes time to hug, I'll grab the little bitch.

Her arms squeezed tight against her sides, and my lips pressed against her ear, I'll say, Marla, you big fake, you get out.

This is the one real thing in my life, and you're wrecking it.

You big tourist.

The next time we meet, I'll say, Marla, I can't sleep with you here. I need this. Get out.

3

YOU WAKE UP at Air Harbor International.

Every takeoff and landing, when the plane banked too much to one side, I prayed for a crash. That moment cures my insomnia with narcolepsy when we might die helpless and packed human tobacco in the fuselage.

This is how I met Tyler Durden.

You wake up at O'Hare.

You wake up at LaGuardia.

You wake up at Logan.

Tyler worked part-time as a movie projectionist. Because of his nature, Tyler could only work night jobs. If a projectionist called in sick, the union called Tyler.

Some people are night people. Some people are day people. I could only work a day job.

You wake up at Dulles.

Life insurance pays off triple if you die on a business trip. I prayed for wind shear effect. I prayed for pelicans sucked into the turbines and loose bolts and ice on the wings. On takeoff, as the plane pushed down the runway and the flaps tilted up, with our seats in their full upright position and our tray tables stowed and all personal carry-on baggage in the overhead compartment, as the end of the runway ran up to meet us with our smoking materials extinguished, I prayed for a crash.

You wake up at Love Field.

In a projection booth, Tyler did changeovers if the theater was old enough. With changeovers, you have two projectors in the booth, and one projector is running.

I know this because Tyler knows this.

The second projector is set up with the next reel of film. Most movies are six or seven small reels of film played in a certain order. Newer theaters, they splice all the reels together into one five-foot reel. This way, you don't have to run two projectors and do changeovers, switch back and forth, reel one, switch, reel two on the other projector, switch, reel three on the first projector.

Switch.

You wake up at SeaTac.

I study the people on the laminated airline seat card. A woman floats in the ocean, her brown hair spread out behind her, her seat cushion clutched to her chest. The eyes are wide open, but the woman doesn't smile or frown. In another picture, people calm as Hindu cows reach up from their seats toward oxygen masks sprung out of the ceiling.

This must be an emergency.

Oh.

We've lost cabin pressure.

Oh.

You wake up, and you're at Willow Run.

Old theater, new theater, to ship a movie to the next theater, Tyler has to break the movie back down to the original six or seven reels. The small reels pack into a pair of hexagonal steel suitcases. Each suitcase has a handle on top. Pick one up, and you'll dislocate a shoulder. They weigh that much.

Tyler's a banquet waiter, waiting tables at a hotel, downtown, and Tyler's a projectionist with the projector operator's union. I don't know how long Tyler had been working on all those nights I couldn't sleep.

The old theaters that run a movie with two projectors, a projectionist has to stand right there to change projectors at the exact second so the audience never sees the break when one reel starts and one reel ran out. You have to look for the white dots in the top, right-hand corner of the screen. This is the warning. Watch the movie, and you'll see two dots at the end of a reel.

"Cigarette burns," they're called in the business.

The first white dot, this is the two-minute warning. You get the second projector started so it will be running up to speed.

The second white dot is the five-second warning. Excitement. You're standing between the two projectors and the booth is sweating hot from the xenon bulbs that if you looked right at them you're blind. The first dot flashes on the screen. The sound in a movie comes from a big speaker behind the screen. The projectionist booth is soundproof because inside the booth is the racket of sprockets snapping film past the lens at six feet a second, ten frames a foot, sixty frames a second snapping through, clattering Gatling-gun fire. The two projectors running, you stand between and hold the shutter lever on each. On really old projectors, you have an alarm on the hub of the feed reel.

Even after the movie's on television, the warning dots will still be there. Even on airplane movies.

As most of the movie rolls onto the take-up reel, the take-up reel turns slower and the feed reel has to turn faster. At the end of a reel, the feed reel turns so fast the alarm will start ringing to warn you that a changeover is coming up.

The dark is hot from the bulbs inside the projectors, and the alarm is ringing. Stand there between the two projectors with a lever in each hand, and watch the corner of the screen. The second dot flashes. Count to five. Switch one shutter closed. At the same time, open the other shutter.

Changeover.

The movie goes on.

Nobody in the audience has any idea.

The alarm is on the feed reel so the movie projectionist can nap. A movie projectionist does a lot he's not supposed to. Not every projector has the alarm. At home, you'll sometimes wake up in your dark bed with the terror you've fallen asleep in the booth and missed a changeover. The audience will be cursing you. The audience, their movie dream is ruined, and the manager will be calling the union.

You wake up at Krissy Field.

The charm of traveling is everywhere I go, tiny life. I go to the hotel, tiny soap, tiny shampoos, single-serving butter, tiny mouthwash and a single-use toothbrush. Fold into the standard airplane seat. You're a giant. The problem is your shoulders are too big. Your Alice in Wonderland legs are all of a sudden miles so long they touch the feet of the person in front. Dinner arrives, a miniature do-it-yourself Chicken Cordon Bleu hobby kit, sort of a put-it-together project to keep you busy.

The pilot has turned on the seat-belt sign, and we would ask you to refrain from moving about the cabin.

You wake up at Meigs Field.

Sometimes, Tyler wakes up in the dark, buzzing with the terror that he's missed a reel change or the movie has broken or the movie has slipped just enough in the projector that the sprockets are punching a line of holes through the sound track.

After a movie has been sprocket run, the light of the bulb shines through the sound track and instead of talk, you're blasted with the helicopter blade sound of *whop whop whop* as each burst of light comes through a sprocket hole.

What else a projectionist shouldn't do: Tyler makes slides out of the best single frames from a movie. The first full frontal movie anyone can remember had the naked actress Angie Dickinson.

By the time a print of this movie had shipped from the West Coast theaters to the East Coast theaters, the nude scene was gone. One projectionist took a frame. Another projectionist took a frame. Everybody wanted to make a naked slide of Angie Dickinson. Porno got into theaters and these projectionists, some guys they built collections that got epic.

You wake up at Boeing Field.

You wake up at LAX.

We have an almost empty flight, tonight, so feel free to fold the armrests up into the seatbacks and stretch out. You stretch out, zigzag, knees bent, waist bent, elbows bent across three or four seats. I set my watch two hours earlier or three hours later, Pacific, Mountain, Central, or Eastern time; lose an hour, gain an hour.

This is your life, and it's ending one minute at a time.

You wake up at Cleveland Hopkins.

You wake up at SeaTac, again.

You're a projectionist and you're tired and angry, but mostly you're bored so you start by taking a single frame of pornography collected by some other projectionist that you find stashed away in the booth, and you splice this frame of a lunging red penis or a yawning wet vagina close-up into another feature movie.

This is one of those pet adventures, when the dog and cat are left behind by a traveling family and must find their way home. In reel three, just after the dog and cat, who have human voices and talk to each other, have eaten out of a garbage can, there's the flash of an erection.

Tyler does this.

A single frame in a movie is on the screen for one-sixtieth of a second. Divide a second into sixty equal parts. That's how long the erection is. Towering four stories tall over the popcorn auditorium, slippery red and terrible, and no one sees it.

You wake up at Logan, again.

This is a terrible way to travel. I go to meetings my boss doesn't want to attend. I take notes. I'll get back to you.

Wherever I'm going, I'll be there to apply the formula. I'll keep the secret intact.

It's simple arithmetic.

It's a story problem.

If a new car built by my company leaves Chicago traveling west at 60 miles per hour, and the rear differential locks up, and the car crashes and burns with everyone trapped inside, does my company initiate a recall?

You take the population of vehicles in the field (A) and multiply it by the probable rate of failure (B), then multiply the result by the average cost of an out-of-court settlement (C).

A times B times C equals X. This is what it will cost if we don't initiate a recall.

If X is greater than the cost of a recall, we recall the cars and no one gets hurt.

If X is less than the cost of a recall, then we don't recall.

Everywhere I go, there's the burned-up wadded-up shell of a car waiting for me. I know where all the skeletons are. Consider this my job security.

Hotel time, restaurant food. Everywhere I go, I make tiny friendships with the people sitting beside me from Logan to Krissy to Willow Run.

What I am is a recall campaign coordinator, I tell the single-serving friend sitting next to me, but I'm working toward a career as a dishwasher.

You wake up at O'Hare, again.

Tyler spliced a penis into everything after that. Usually, close-ups, or a Grand Canyon vagina with an echo, four stories tall and twitching with blood pressure as Cinderella danced with her Prince Charming and people watched. Nobody complained. People ate and drank, but the evening wasn't the same. People feel sick or start to cry and don't know why. Only a hummingbird could have caught Tyler at work.

You wake up at JFK.

I melt and swell at the moment of landing when one wheel thuds on the runway but the plane leans to one side and hangs in the decision to right itself or roll. For this moment, nothing matters. Look up into the stars and you're gone. Not your luggage. Nothing matters. Not your bad breath. The windows are dark outside and the turbine engines roar backward. The cabin hangs at the wrong angle under the roar of the turbines, and you will never have to file another expense account claim. Receipt required for items over twenty-five dollars. You will never have to get another haircut.

A thud, and the second wheel hits the tarmac. The staccato of a hundred seat-belt buckles snapping open, and the single-use friend you almost died sitting next to says:

I hope you make your connection.

Yeah, me too.

And this is how long your moment lasted. And life goes on.

And somehow, by accident, Tyler and I met.

It was time for a vacation.

You wake up at LAX.

Again.

How I met Tyler was I went to a nude beach. This was the very end of summer, and I was asleep. Tyler was naked and sweating, gritty with sand, his hair wet and stringy, hanging in his face.

Tyler had been around a long time before we met.

Tyler was pulling driftwood logs out of the surf and dragging them up the beach. In the wet sand, he'd already planted a half circle of logs so they stood a few inches apart and as tall as his eyes. There were four logs, and when I woke up, I watched Tyler pull a fifth log up the beach. Tyler dug a hole under one end of the log, then lifted the other end until the log slid into the hole and stood there at a slight angle.

You wake up at the beach.

We were the only people on the beach.

With a stick, Tyler drew a straight line in the sand several feet away. Tyler went back to straighten the log by stamping sand around its base.

I was the only person watching this.

Tyler called over, "Do you know what time it is?"

I always wear a watch.

"Do you know what time it is?"

I asked, where?

"Right here," Tyler said. "Right now."

It was 4:06 P.M.

After a while, Tyler sat cross-legged in the shadow of the standing logs. Tyler sat for a few minutes, got up and took a swim, pulled on a T-shirt and a pair of sweatpants, and started to leave. I had to ask.

I had to know what Tyler was doing while I was asleep.

If I could wake up in a different place, at a different time, could I wake up as a different person?

I asked if Tyler was an artist.

Tyler shrugged and showed me how the five standing logs were wider at the base. Tyler showed me the line he'd drawn in the sand, and how he'd use the line to gauge the shadow cast by each log.

Sometimes, you wake up and have to ask where you are.

What Tyler had created was the shadow of a giant hand. Only now the fingers were Nosferatu-long and the thumb was too short, but he said how at exactly four-thirty the hand was perfect. The giant shadow hand was perfect for one minute, and for one perfect minute Tyler had sat in the palm of a perfection he'd created himself.

You wake up, and you're nowhere.

One minute was enough, Tyler said, a person had to work hard for it, but a minute of perfection was worth the effort. A moment was the most you could ever expect from perfection.

You wake up, and that's enough.

His name was Tyler Durden, and he was a movie projectionist with the union, and he was a banquet waiter at a hotel, downtown, and he gave me his phone number.

And this is how we met.

4

ALL THE USUAL brain parasites are here, tonight. Above and Beyond always gets a big turnout. This is Peter. This is Aldo. This is Marcy.

Hi.

The introductions, Everybody, this is Marla Singer, and this is her first time with us.

Hi, Marla.

At Above and Beyond, we start with the Catch-Up Rap. The group isn't called Parasitic Brain Parasites. You'll never hear anyone say "parasite." Everybody is always getting better. Oh, this new medication. Everyone's always just turned the corner. Still, everywhere, there's the squint of a five-day headache. A woman wipes at involuntary tears. Everyone gets a name tag, and people you've met every Tuesday night for a year, they come at you, handshake hand ready and their eyes on your name tag.

I don't believe we've met.

No one will ever say *parasite*. They'll say, *agent*.

They don't say *cure*. They'll say, *treatment*.

In Catch-Up Rap, someone will say how the agent has spread into his spinal column and now all of a sudden he'll have no control of his left hand. The agent, someone will say, has dried the lining of his brain so now the brain pulls away from the inside of his skull, causing seizures.

The last time I was here, the woman named Chloe announced the only good news she had. Chloe pushed herself to her feet against the wooden arms of her chair and said she no longer had any fear of death.

Tonight, after the introductions and Catch-Up Rap, a girl I don't know, with a name tag that says Glenda, says she's Chloe's sister and that at two in the morning last Tuesday, Chloe finally died.

Oh, this should be so sweet. For two years, Chloe's been crying in my arms during hug time, and now she's dead, dead in the ground, dead in an urn, mausoleum, columbarium. Oh, the proof that one day you're thinking and hauling yourself around, and the next, you're cold fertilizer, worm buffet. This is the amazing miracle of death, and it should be so sweet if it weren't for, oh, that one.

Marla.

Oh, and Marla's looking at me again, singled out among all the brain parasites.

Liar.

Faker.

Marla's the faker. You're the faker. Everyone around when they wince or twitch and fall down barking and the crotch of their jeans turns dark blue, well, it's all just a big act.

Guided meditation all of a sudden won't take me anywhere, tonight. Behind each of the seven palace doors, the green door, the orange door, Marla. The blue door, Marla stands there. Liar. In the guided meditation through the cave of my power animal, my power animal is Marla. Smoking her cigarette, Marla, rolling her eyes. Liar. Black hair and pillowy French lips. Faker. Italian dark leather sofa lips. You can't escape.

Chloe was the genuine article.

Chloe was the way Joni Mitchell's skeleton would look if you made it smile and walk around a party being extra special nice to everyone. Picture Chloe's popular skeleton the size of an insect, running through the vaults and galleries of her innards at two in the morning. Her pulse a siren overhead, announcing: Prepare for death in ten, in nine, in eight seconds. Death will commence in seven, six . . .

At night, Chloe ran around the maze of her own collapsing veins and burst tubes spraying hot lymph. Nerves surface as trip wires in the tissue. Abscesses swell in the tissue around her as hot white pearls.

The overhead announcement, prepare to evacuate bowels in ten, in nine, eight, seven.

Prepare to evacuate soul in ten, in nine, eight.

Chloe's splashing through the ankle-deep backup of renal fluid from her failed kidneys.

Death will commence in five.

Five, four.

Four.

Around her, parasitic life spray paints her heart.

Four, three.

Three, two.

Chloe climbs hand-over-hand up the curdled lining of her own throat.

Death to commence in three, in two.

Moonlight shines in through the open mouth.

Prepare for the last breath, now.

Evacuate.

Now.

Soul clear of body.

Now.

Death commences.

Now.

Oh, this should be so sweet, the remembered warm jumble of Chloe still in my arms and Chloe dead somewhere.

But no, I'm watched by Marla.

In guided meditation, I open my arms to receive my inner child, and the child is Marla smoking her cigarette. No white healing ball of light. Liar. No chakras. Picture your chakras opening as flowers and at the center of each is a slow-motion explosion of sweet light.

Liar.

My chakras stay closed.

When meditation ends, everyone is stretching and twisting their heads and pulling each other to their feet in preparation. Therapeutic physical contact. For the hug, I cross in three steps to stand against Marla who looks up into my face as I watch everyone else for the cue.

Let's all, the cue comes, embrace someone near us.

My arms clamp around Marla.

Pick someone special to you, tonight.

Marla's cigarette hands are pinned to her waist.

Tell this someone how you feel.

Marla doesn't have testicular cancer. Marla doesn't have tuberculosis. She isn't dying. Okay in that brainy brain-food philosophy way, we're all dying, but Marla isn't dying the way Chloe was dying.

The cue comes, share yourself.

So, Marla, how do you like them apples?

Share yourself completely.

So, Marla, get out. Get out. Get out.

Go ahead and cry if you have to.

Marla stares up at me. Her eyes are brown. Her earlobes pucker around earring holes, no earrings. Her chapped lips are frosted with dead skin.

Go ahead and cry.

"You're not dying either," Marla says.

Around us, couples stand sobbing, propped against each other.

"You tell on me," Marla says, "and I'll tell on you."

Then we can split the week, I say. Marla can have bone disease, brain parasites, and tuberculosis. I'll keep testicular cancer, blood parasites, and organic brain dementia.

Marla says, "What about ascending bowel cancers?"

The girl has done her homework.

We'll split bowel cancer. She gets it the first and third Sunday of every month.

"No," Marla says. No, she wants it all. The cancers, the parasites. Marla's eyes narrow. She never dreamed she could feel so 'smarvelous. She actually felt alive. Her skin was clearing up. All her life, she never saw a dead person. There was no real sense of life because she had nothing to contrast it with. Oh, but now there was dying and death and loss and grief. Weeping and shuddering, terror and remorse. Now that she knows where we're all going, Marla feels every moment of her life.

No, she wasn't leaving any group.

"Not and go back to the way life felt before," Marla says. "I used to work in a funeral home to feel good about myself, just the fact I was breathing. So what if I couldn't get a job in my field."

Then go back to your funeral home, I say.

"Funerals are nothing compared to this," Marla says. "Funerals are all abstract ceremony. Here, you have a real experience of death."

Couples around the two of us are drying their tears, sniffing, patting each other on the back and letting go.

We can't both come, I tell her.

"Then don't come."

I need this.

"Then go to funerals."

Everyone else has broken apart and they're joining hands for the closing prayer. I let Marla go.

"How long have you been coming here?"

The closing prayer.

Two years.

A man in the prayer circle takes my hand. A man takes Marla's hand.

These prayers start and usually, my breathing is blown. Oh, bless us. Oh, bless us in our anger and our fear.

"Two years?" Marla tilts her head to whisper.

Oh, bless us and hold us.

Anyone who might've noticed me in two years has either died or recovered and never came back.

Help us and help us.

"Okay," Marla says, "okay, okay, you can have testicular cancer."

Big Bob the big cheesebread crying all over me. Thanks.

Bring us to our destiny. Bring us peace.

"Don't mention it."

This is how I met Marla.

5

THE SECURITY TASK force guy explained everything to me.

Baggage handlers can ignore a ticking suitcase. The security task force guy, he called baggage handlers Throwers. Modern bombs don't tick. But a suitcase that vibrates, the baggage handlers, the Throwers, have to call the police.

How I came to live with Tyler is because most airlines have this policy about vibrating baggage.

My flight back from Dulles, I had everything in that one bag. When you travel a lot, you learn to pack the same for every trip. Six white shirts. Two black trousers. The bare minimum you need to survive.

Traveling alarm clock.

Cordless electric razor.

Toothbrush.

Six pair underwear.

Six pair black socks.

It turns out, my suitcase was vibrating on departure from Dulles, according to the security task force guy, so the police took it off the flight. Everything was in that bag. My contact lens stuff. One red tie with blue stripes. One blue tie with red stripes. These are regimental stripes, not club tie stripes. And one solid red tie.

A list of all these things used to hang on the inside of my bedroom door at home.

Home was a condominium on the fifteenth floor of a high-rise, a sort of filing cabinet for widows and young professionals. The marketing brochure promised a foot of concrete floor, ceiling, and wall between me and any adjacent stereo or turned-up television. A foot of concrete and air conditioning, you couldn't open the windows so even with maple flooring and dimmer switches, all seventeen hundred airtight feet would smell like the last meal you cooked or your last trip to the bathroom.

Yeah, and there were butcher block countertops and low-voltage track lighting.

Still, a foot of concrete is important when your next-door neighbor lets the battery on her hearing aid go and has to watch her game shows at full blast. Or when a volcanic blast of burning gas and debris that used to be your living-room set and personal effects blows out your floor-to-ceiling windows and sails down flaming to leave just your condo, only yours, a gutted charred concrete hole in the cliffside of the building.

These things happen.

Everything, including your set of hand-blown green glass dishes with the tiny bubbles and imperfections, little bits of sand, proof they were crafted by the honest, simple, hard-working indigenous aboriginal peoples of wherever, well, these dishes all get blown out by the blast. Picture the floor-to-ceiling drapes blown out and flaming to shreds in the hot wind.

Fifteen floors over the city, this stuff comes flaming and bashing and shattering down on everyone's car.

Me, while I'm heading west, asleep at Mach 0.83 or 455 miles an hour, true airspeed, the FBI is bomb-squading my suitcase on a vacated runway back at Dulles. Nine times out of ten, the security task force guy says, the vibration is an electric razor. This was my cordless electric razor. The other time, it's a vibrating dildo.

The security task force guy told me this. This was at my destination, without my suitcase, where I was about to cab it home and find my flannel sheets shredded on the ground.

Imagine, the task force guy says, telling a passenger on arrival that a dildo kept her baggage on the East Coast. Sometimes it's even a man. It's airline policy not to imply ownership in the event of a dildo. Use the indefinite article.

A dildo.

Never your dildo.

Never, ever say the dildo accidentally turned itself on.

A dildo activated itself and created an emergency situation that required evacuating your baggage.

Rain was falling when I woke up for my connection in Stapleton.

Rain was falling when I woke up on our final approach to home.

An announcement told us to please take this opportunity to check around our seats for any personal belongings we might have left behind. Then the announcement said my name. Would I please meet with an airline representative waiting at the gate.

I set my watch back three hours, and it was still after midnight.

There was the airline representative at the gate, and there was the security task force guy to say, ha, your electric razor kept your checked baggage at Dulles. The task force guy called the baggage handlers

Throwers. Then he called them Rampers. To prove things could be worse, the guy told me at least it wasn't a dildo. Then, maybe because I'm a guy and he's a guy and it's one o'clock in the morning, maybe to make me laugh, the guy said industry slang for flight attendant was Space Waitress. Or Air Mattress. It looked like the guy was wearing a pilot's uniform, white shirt with little epaulets and a blue tie. My luggage had been cleared, he said, and would arrive the next day.

The security guy asked my name and address and phone number, and then he asked me what was the difference between a condom and a cockpit.

"You can only get one prick into a condom," he said.

I cabbed home on my last ten bucks.

The local police had been asking a lot of questions, too.

My electric razor, which wasn't a bomb, was still three time zones behind me.

Something which was a bomb, a big bomb, had blasted my clever Njurunda coffee tables in the shape of a lime green yin and an orange yang that fit together to make a circle. Well they were splinters, now.

My Haparanda sofa group with the orange slip covers, design by Erika Pekkari, it was trash, now.

And I wasn't the only slave to my nesting instinct. The people I know who used to sit in the bathroom with pornography, now they sit in the bathroom with their IKEA furniture catalogue.

We all have the same Johanneshov armchair in the Strinne green stripe pattern. Mine fell fifteen stories, burning, into a fountain.

We all have the same Rislampa/Har paper lamps made from wire and environmentally friendly unbleached paper. Mine are confetti.

All that sitting in the bathroom.

The Alle cutlery service. Stainless steel. Dishwasher safe.

The Vild hall clock made of galvanized steel, oh, I had to have that.

The Klipsk shelving unit, oh, yeah.

Hemlig hat boxes. Yes.

The street outside my high-rise was sparkling and scattered with all this.

The Mommala quilt-cover set. Design by Tomas Harila and available in the following:

Orchid.

Fuschia.

Cobalt.

Ebony.

Jet.

Eggshell or heather.

It took my whole life to buy this stuff.

The easy-care textured lacquer of my Kalix occasional tables.

My Steg nesting tables.

You buy furniture. You tell yourself, this is the last sofa I will ever need in my life. Buy the sofa, then for a couple years you're satisfied that no matter what goes wrong, at least you've got your sofa issue handled. Then the right set of dishes. Then the perfect bed. The drapes. The rug.

Then you're trapped in your lovely nest, and the things you used to own, now they own you.

Until I got home from the airport.

The doorman steps out of the shadows to say, there's been an accident. The police, they were here and asked a lot of questions.

The police think maybe it was the gas. Maybe the pilot light on the stove went out or a burner was left on, leaking gas, and the gas rose to the ceiling, and the gas filled the condo from ceiling to floor in every room. The condo was seventeen hundred square feet with high ceilings and for days and days, the gas must've leaked until every room was full. When the rooms were filled to the floor, the compressor at the base of the refrigerator clicked on.

Detonation.

The floor-to-ceiling windows in their aluminum frames went out and the sofas and the lamps and dishes and sheet sets in flames, and the high school annuals and the diplomas and telephone. Everything blasting out from the fifteenth floor in a sort of solar flare.

Oh, not my refrigerator. I'd collected shelves full of different mustards, some stone-ground, some English pub style. There were fourteen different flavors of fat-free salad dressing, and seven kinds of capers.

I know, I know, a house full of condiments and no real food.

The doorman blew his nose and something went into his handkerchief with the good slap of a pitch into a catcher's mitt.

You could go up to the fifteen floor, the doorman said, but nobody could go into the unit. Police orders. The police had been asking, did I have an old girlfriend who'd want to do this or did I make an enemy of somebody who had access to dynamite.

"It wasn't worth going up," the doorman said. "All that's left is the concrete shell."

The police hadn't ruled out arson. No one had smelled gas. The doorman raises an eyebrow. This guy spent his time flirting with the day maids and nurses who worked in the big units on the top floor and waited in the lobby chairs for their rides after work. Three years I lived here, and the doorman still sat reading his *Ellery Queen* magazine every night while I shifted packages and bags to unlock the front door and let myself in.

The doorman raises an eyebrow and says how some people will go on a long trip and leave a candle, a long, long candle burning in a big puddle of gasoline. People with financial difficulties do this stuff. People who want out from under.

I asked to use the lobby phone.

"A lot of young people try to impress the world and buy too many things," the doorman said.

I called Tyler.

The phone rang in Tyler's rented house on Paper Street.

Oh, Tyler, please deliver me.

And the phone rang.

The doorman leaned into my shoulder and said, "A lot of young people don't know what they really want."

Oh, Tyler, please rescue me.

And the phone rang.

"Young people, they think they want the whole world."

Deliver me from Swedish furniture.

Deliver me from clever art.

And the phone rang and Tyler answered.

"If you don't know what you want," the doorman said, "you end up with a lot you don't."

May I never be complete.

May I never be content.

May I never be perfect.

Deliver me, Tyler, from being perfect and complete.

Tyler and I agreed to meet at a bar.

The doorman asked for a number where the police could reach me. It was still raining. My Audi was still parked in the lot, but a Dakapo halogen torchiere was speared through the windshield.

Tyler and I, we met and drank a lot of beer, and Tyler said, yes, I could move in with him, but I would have to do him a favor.

The next day, my suitcase would arrive with the bare minimum, six shirts, six pair of underwear.

There, drunk in a bar where no one was watching and no one would care, I asked Tyler what he wanted me to do.

Tyler said, "I want you to hit me as hard as you can."

6

TWO SCREENS INTO my demo to Microsoft, I taste blood and have to start swallowing. My boss doesn't know the material, but he won't let me run the demo with a black eye and half my face swollen from the stitches inside my cheek. The stitches have come loose, and I can feel them with my tongue against the inside of my cheek. Picture snarled fishing line on the beach. I can picture them as the black stitches on a dog after it's been fixed, and I keep swallowing blood. My boss is making the presentation from my script, and I'm running the laptop projector so I'm off to one side of the room, in the dark.

More of my lips are sticky with blood as I try to lick the blood off, and when the lights come up, I will turn to consultants Ellen and Walter and Norbert and Linda from Microsoft and say, thank you for coming, my mouth shining with blood and blood climbing the cracks between my teeth.

You can swallow about a pint of blood before you're sick.

Fight club is tomorrow, and I'm not going to miss fight club.

Before the presentation, Walter from Microsoft smiles his steam shovel jaw like a marketing tool tanned the color of a barbecued potato chip. Walter with his signet ring shakes my hand, wrapped in his smooth soft hand and says, "I'd hate to see what happened to the other guy."

The first rule about fight club is you don't talk about fight club.

I tell Walter I fell.

I did this to myself.

Before the presentation, when I sat across from my boss, telling him where in the script each slide cues and when I wanted to run the video segment, my boss says, "What do you get yourself into every weekend?"

I just don't want to die without a few scars, I say. It's nothing anymore to have a beautiful stock body. You see those cars that are completely stock cherry, right out of a dealer's showroom in 1955, I always think, what a waste.

The second rule about fight club is you don't talk about fight club.

Maybe at lunch, the waiter comes to your table and the waiter has the two black eyes of a giant panda from fight club last weekend when you saw him get his head pinched between the concrete floor and the knee of a two-hundred-pound stock boy who kept slamming a fist into the bridge of the waiter's nose again and again in flat hard packing sounds you could hear over all the yelling until the waiter caught enough breath and sprayed blood to say, stop.

You don't say anything because fight club exists only in the hours between when fight club starts and when fight club ends.

You saw the kid who works in the copy center, a month ago you saw this kid who can't remember to three-hole-punch an order or put colored slip sheets between the copy packets, but this kid was a god for ten minutes when you saw him kick the air out of an account representative twice his size then land on the man and pound him limp until the kid had to stop. That's the third rule in fight club, when someone says stop, or goes limp, even if he's just faking it, the fight is over. Every time you see this kid, you can't tell him what a great fight he had.

Only two guys to a fight. One fight at a time. They fight without shirts or shoes. The fights go on as long as they have to. Those are the other rules of fight club.

Who guys are in fight club is not who they are in the real world. Even if you told the kid in the copy center that he had a good fight, you wouldn't be talking to the same man.

Who I am in fight club is not someone my boss knows.

After a night in fight club, everything in the real world gets the volume turned down. Nothing can piss you off. Your word is law, and if other people break that law or question you, even that doesn't piss you off.

In the real world, I'm a recall campaign coordinator in a shirt and tie, sitting in the dark with a mouthful of blood and changing the overheads and slides as my boss tells Microsoft how he chose a particular shade of pale cornflower blue for an icon.

The first fight club was just Tyler and I pounding on each other.

It used to be enough that when I came home angry and knowing that my life wasn't toeing my five-year plan, I could clean my condominium or detail my car. Someday I'd be dead without a scar and there would be a really nice condo and car. Really, really nice, until the dust settled or the next owner. Nothing is static. Even the *Mona Lisa* is falling apart. Since fight club, I can wiggle half the teeth in my jaw.

Maybe self-improvement isn't the answer.

Tyler never knew his father.

Maybe self-destruction is the answer.

Tyler and I still go to fight club, together. Fight club is in the basement of a bar, now, after the bar closes on Saturday night, and every week you go and there's more guys there.

Tyler gets under the one light in the middle of the black concrete basement and he can see that light flickering back out of the dark in a hundred pairs of eyes. First thing Tyler yells is, "The first rule about fight club is you don't talk about fight club.

"The second rule about fight club," Tyler yells, "is you don't talk about fight club."

Me, I knew my dad for about six years, but I don't remember anything. My dad, he starts a new family in a new town about every six years. This isn't so much like a family as it's like he sets up a franchise.

What you see at fight club is a generation of men raised by women.

Tyler standing under the one light in the after-midnight blackness of a basement full of men, Tyler runs through the other rules: two men per fight, one fight at a time, no shoes no shirts, fights go on as long as they have to.

"And the seventh rule," Tyler yells, "is if this is your first night at fight club, you have to fight."

Fight club is not football on television. You aren't watching a bunch of men you don't know halfway around the world beating on each other live by satellite with a two-minute delay, commercials pitching beer every ten minutes, and a pause now for station identification. After you've been to fight club, watching football on television is watching pornography when you could be having great sex.

Fight club gets to be your reason for going to the gym and keeping your hair cut short and cutting your nails. The gyms you go to are crowded with guys trying to look like men, as if being a man means looking the way a sculptor or an art director says.

Like Tyler says, even a soufflé looks pumped.

My father never went to college so it was really important I go to college. After college, I called him long distance and said, now what?

My dad didn't know.

When I got a job and turned twenty-five, long distance, I said, now what? My dad didn't know, so he said, get married.

I'm a thirty-year-old boy, and I'm wondering if another woman is really the answer I need.

What happens at fight club doesn't happen in words. Some guys need a fight every week. This week, Tyler says it's the first fifty guys through the door and that's it. No more.

Last week, I tapped a guy and he and I got on the list for a fight. This guy must've had a bad week, got both my arms behind my head in a full nelson and rammed my face into the concrete floor until my teeth bit open the inside of my cheek and my eye was swollen shut and was bleeding, and after I said, stop, I could look down and there was a print of half my face in blood on the floor.

Tyler stood next to me, both of us looking down at the big O of my mouth with blood all around it and the little slit of my eye staring up at us from the floor, and Tyler says, "Cool."

I shake the guy's hand and say, good fight.

This guy, he says, "How about next week?"

I try to smile against all the swelling, and I say, look at me. How about next month?

You aren't alive anywhere like you're alive at fight club. When it's you and one other guy under that one light in the middle of all those watching. Fight club isn't about winning or losing fights. Fight club isn't about words. You see a guy come to fight club for the first time, and his ass is a loaf of white bread. You see this same guy here six months later, and he looks carved out of wood. This guy trusts himself to handle anything. There's grunting and noise at fight club like at the gym, but fight club isn't about looking good. There's hysterical shouting in tongues like at church, and when you wake up Sunday afternoon you feel saved.

After my last fight, the guy who fought me mopped the floor while I called my insurance to pre-approve a visit to the emergency room. At the hospital, Tyler tells them I fell down.

Sometimes, Tyler speaks for me.

I did this to myself.

Outside, the sun was coming up.

You don't talk about fight club because except for five hours from two until seven on Sunday morning, fight club doesn't exist.

When we invented fight club, Tyler and I, neither of us had ever been in a fight before. If you've never been in a fight, you wonder. About getting hurt, about what you're capable of doing against another man. I was the first guy Tyler ever felt safe enough to ask, and we were both drunk in a bar where no one would care so Tyler said, "I want you to do me a favor. I want you to hit me as hard as you can."

I didn't want to, but Tyler explained it all, about not wanting to die without any scars, about being tired of watching only professionals fight, and wanting to know more about himself.

About self-destruction.

At the time, my life just seemed too complete, and maybe we have to break everything to make something better out of ourselves.

I looked around and said, okay. Okay, I say, but outside in the parking lot.

So we went outside, and I asked if Tyler wanted it in the face or in the stomach.

Tyler said, "Surprise me."

I said I had never hit anybody.

Tyler said, "So go crazy, man."

I said, close your eyes.

Tyler said, "No."

Like every guy on his first night in fight club, I breathed in and swung my fist in a roundhouse at Tyler's jaw like in every cowboy movie we'd ever seen, and me, my fist connected with the side of Tyler's neck.

Shit, I said, that didn't count. I want to try it again.

Tyler said, "Yeah it counted," and hit me, straight on, *pow,* just like a cartoon boxing glove on a spring on Saturday morning cartoons, right in the middle of my chest and I fell back against a car. We both stood there, Tyler rubbing the side of his neck and me holding a hand on my chest, both of us knowing we'd gotten somewhere we'd never been and like the cat and mouse in cartoons, we were still alive and wanted to see how far we could take this thing and still be alive.

Tyler said, "Cool."

I said, hit me again.

Tyler said, "No, you hit me."

So I hit him, a girl's wide roundhouse to right under his ear, and Tyler shoved me back and stomped the heel of his shoe in my stomach. What happened next and after that didn't happen in words, but the bar closed and people came out and shouted around us in the parking lot.

Instead of Tyler, I felt finally I could get my hands on everything in the world that didn't work, my cleaning that came back with the collar buttons broken, the bank that says I'm hundreds of dollars overdrawn. My job where my boss got on my computer and fiddled with my DOS execute commands. And Marla Singer, who stole the support groups from me.

Nothing was solved when the fight was over, but nothing mattered.

The first night we fought was a Sunday night, and Tyler hadn't shaved all weekend so my knuckles burned raw from his weekend beard. Lying on our backs in the parking lot, staring up at the one star that came through the streetlights, I asked Tyler what he'd been fighting.

Tyler said, his father.

Maybe we didn't need a father to complete ourselves. There's nothing personal about who you fight in fight club. You fight to fight. You're not supposed to talk about fight club, but we talked and for the next couple of weeks, guys met in that parking lot after the bar had closed, and by the time it got cold, another bar offered the basement where we meet now.

When fight club meets, Tyler gives the rules he and I decided. "Most of you," Tyler yells in the cone of light in the center of the basement full of men, "you're here because someone broke the rules. Somebody told you about fight club."

Tyler says, "Well, you better stop talking or you'd better start another fight club because next week you put your name on a list when you get here, and only the first fifty names on the list get in. If you get in, you set up your fight right away if you want a fight. If you don't want a fight, there are guys who do, so maybe you should just stay home.

"If this is your first night at fight club," Tyler yells, "you have to fight."

Most guys are at fight club because of something they're too scared to fight. After a few fights, you're afraid a lot less.

A lot of best friends meet for the first time at fight club. Now I go to meetings or conferences and see faces at conference tables, accountants and junior executives or attorneys with broken noses spreading out like an eggplant under the edges of bandages or they have a couple stitches under an eye or a jaw wired shut. These are the quiet young men who listen until it's time to decide.

We nod to each other.

Later, my boss will ask me how I know so many of these guys.

According to my boss, there are fewer and fewer gentlemen in business and more thugs.

The demo goes on.

Walter from Microsoft catches my eye. Here's a young guy with perfect teeth and clear skin and the kind of job you bother to write the alumni magazine about getting. You know he was too young to fight in any wars, and if his parents weren't divorced, his father was never home, and here he's looking at me with half my face clean shaved and half a leering bruise hidden in the dark. Blood shining on my lips. And maybe Walter's thinking about a meatless, pain-free potluck he went to last weekend or the ozone or the Earth's desperate need to stop cruel product testing on animals, but probably he's not.

7

ONE MORNING, THERE'S the dead jellyfish of a used condom floating in the toilet.

This is how Tyler meets Marla.

I get up to take a leak, and there against the sort of cave paintings of dirt in the toilet bowl is this. You have to wonder, what do sperm think.

This?

This is the vaginal vault?

What's happening here?

All night long, I dreamed I was humping Marla Singer. Marla Singer smoking her cigarette. Marla Singer rolling her eyes. I wake up alone in my own bed, and the door to Tyler's room is closed. The door to Tyler's room is never closed. All night, it was raining. The shingles on the roof blister, buckle, curl, and the rain comes through and collects on top of the ceiling plaster and drips down through the light fixtures.

When it's raining, we have to pull the fuses. You don't dare turn on the lights. The house that Tyler rents, it has three stories and a basement. We carry around candles. It has pantries and screened sleeping porches and stained-glass windows on the stairway landing. There are bay windows with window seats in the parlor. The baseboard moldings are carved and varnished and eighteen inches high.

The rain trickles down through the house, and everything wooden swells and shrinks, and the nails in everything wooden, the floors and baseboards and window casings, the nails inch out and rust.

Everywhere there are rusted nails to step on or snag your elbow on, and there's only one bathroom for the seven bedrooms, and now there's a used condom.

The house is waiting for something, a zoning change or a will to come out of probate, and then it will be torn down. I asked Tyler how long he's been here, and he said about six weeks. Before the dawn of time, there was an owner who collected lifetime stacks of the *National Geographic* and *Reader's Digest*. Big teetering stacks of magazines that get taller every time it rains. Tyler says the last tenant used to fold the glossy magazine pages for cocaine envelopes. There's no lock on the front door from when police or whoever kicked in the door. There's nine layers of wallpaper swelling on the dining-room walls, flowers under stripes under flowers under birds under grasscloth.

Our only neighbors are a closed machine shop and across the street, a block-long warehouse. Inside the house, there's a closet with seven-foot rollers for rolling up damask tablecloths so they never have to be creased. There's a cedar-lined, refrigerated fur closet. The tile in the bathroom is painted with little flowers nicer than most everybody's wedding china, and there's a used condom in the toilet.

I've been living with Tyler about a month.

Tyler comes to breakfast with hickies sucked all over his neck and chest, and I'm reading through an old *Reader's Digest* magazine. This is the perfect house for dealing drugs. There are no neighbors. There's nothing else on Paper Street except for warehouses and the pulp mill. The fart smell of steam from the paper mill, and the hamster cage smell of wood chips in orange pyramids around the mill. This is the perfect house for dealing drugs because a bah-zillion trucks drive down Paper Street everyday, but at night, Tyler and I are alone for a half mile in every direction.

I found stacks and stacks of *Reader's Digest* in the basement and now there's a pile of *Reader's Digest* in every room.

Life in These United States.

Laughter Is the Best Medicine.

Stacks of magazines are about the only furniture.

In the oldest magazines, there's a series of articles where organs in the human body talk about themselves in the first person: I am Jane's Uterus.

I am Joe's Prostate.

No kidding, and Tyler comes to the kitchen table with his hickies and no shirt and says, blah, blah, blah, blah, blah, he met Marla Singer last night and they had sex.

Hearing this, I am totally Joe's Gallbladder. All of this is my fault. Sometimes you do something, and you get screwed. Sometimes it's the things you don't do, and you get screwed.

Last night, I called Marla. We've worked out a system so if I want to go to a support group, I can call Marla and see if she's planning to go. Melanoma was last night, and I felt a little down.

Marla lives at the Regent Hotel, which is nothing but brown bricks held together with sleaze, where all the mattresses are sealed inside slippery plastic covers, so many people go there to die. You sit on any bed the wrong way, and you and the sheets and blanket slide right to the floor.

I called Marla at the Regent Hotel to see if she was going to Melanoma.

Marla answered in slow motion. This wasn't a for-real suicide, Marla said, this was probably just one of those cry-for-help things, but she had taken too many Xanax.

Picture going over to the Regent Hotel to watch Marla throw herself around her crummy room saying: I'm dying. Dying. I'm dying. Dying. Die-ing. Dying.

This would go on for hours.

So she was staying home tonight, right?

She was doing the big death thing, Marla told me. I should get a move on if I wanted to watch.

Thanks anyway, I said, but I had other plans.

That's okay, Marla said, she could die just as well watching television. Marla just hoped there was something worth watching.

And I ran off to Melanoma. I came home early. I slept.

And now, at breakfast the next morning, Tyler's sitting here covered in hickies and says Marla is some twisted bitch, but he likes that a lot.

After Melanoma last night, I came home and went to bed and slept. And dreamed I was humping, humping, humping Marla Singer.

And this morning, listening to Tyler, I pretend to read the *Reader's Digest*. A twisted bitch, I could've told you that. *Reader's Digest*. Humor in Uniform.

I am Joe's Raging Bile Duct.

The things Marla said to him last night, Tyler says. No girl's ever talked to him that way.

I am Joe's Grinding Teeth.

I am Joe's Inflamed Flaring Nostrils.

After Tyler and Marla had sex about ten times, Tyler says, Marla said she wanted to get pregnant. Marla said she wanted to have Tyler's abortion.

I am Joe's White Knuckles.

How could Tyler not fall for that. The night before last, Tyler sat up alone, splicing sex organs into *Snow White*.

How could I compete for Tyler's attention.

I am Joe's Enraged, Inflamed Sense of Rejection.

What's worse is this is all my fault. After I went to sleep last night, Tyler tells me he came home from his shift as a banquet waiter, and Marla called again from the Regent Hotel. This was it, Marla said. The tunnel, the light leading her down the tunnel. The death experience was so cool, Marla wanted me to hear her describe it as she lifted out of her body and floated up.

Marla didn't know if her spirit could use the telephone, but she wanted someone to at least hear her last breath.

No, but no, Tyler answers the phone and misunderstands the whole situation.

They've never met so Tyler thinks it's a bad thing that Marla is about to die.

It's nothing of the kind.

This is none of Tyler's business, but Tyler calls the police and Tyler races over to the Regent Hotel.

Now, according to the ancient Chinese custom we all learned from television, Tyler is responsible for Marla, forever, because Tyler saved Marla's life.

If I had only wasted a couple of minutes and gone over to watch Marla die, then none of this would have happened.

Tyler tells me how Marla lives in room 8G, on the top floor of the Regent Hotel, up eight flights of stairs and down a noisy hallway with canned television laughter coming through the doors. Every couple seconds an actress screams or actors die screaming in a rattle of bullets. Tyler gets to the end of the hallway and even before he knocks a thin, thin, buttermilk sallow arm slingshots out the door of room 8G, grabs his wrist, and yanks Tyler inside.

I bury myself in a *Reader's Digest*.

Even as Marla yanks Tyler into her room, Tyler can hear brake squeals and sirens collecting out in front of the Regent Hotel. On the dresser, there's a dildo made of the same soft pink plastic as a million Barbie dolls, and for a moment, Tyler can picture millions of baby dolls and Barbie dolls and dildos injection-molded and coming off the same assembly line in Taiwan.

Marla looks at Tyler looking at her dildo, and she rolls her eyes and says, "Don't be afraid. It's not a threat to you."

Marla shoves Tyler back out into the hallway, and she says she's sorry, but he shouldn't have called the police and that's probably the police downstairs right now.

In the hallway, Marla locks the door to 8G and shoves Tyler toward the stairs. On the stairs, Tyler and Marla flatten against the wall as police and paramedics charge by with oxygen, asking which door will be 8G.

Marla tells them the door at the end of the hall.

Marla shouts to the police that the girl who lives in 8G used to be a lovely charming girl, but the girl is a monster bitch monster. The girl is infectious human waste, and she's confused and afraid to commit to the wrong thing so she won't commit to anything.

"The girl in 8G has no faith in herself," Marla shouts, "and she's worried that as she grows older, she'll have fewer and fewer options."

Marla shouts, "Good luck."

The police pile up at the locked door to 8G, and Marla and Tyler hurry down to the lobby. Behind them, a policeman is yelling at the door:

"Let us help you! Miss Singer, you have every reason to live! Just let us in, Marla, and we can help you with your problems!"

Marla and Tyler rushed out into the street. Tyler got Marla into a cab, and high up on the eighth floor of the hotel, Tyler could see shadows moving back and forth across the windows of Marla's room.

Out on the freeway with all the lights and the other cars, six lanes of traffic racing toward the vanishing point, Marla tells Tyler he has to keep her up all night. If Marla ever falls asleep, she'll die.

A lot of people wanted Marla dead, she told Tyler. These people were already dead and on the other side, and at night they called on the telephone. Marla would go to bars and hear the bartender calling her name, and when she took the call, the line was dead.

Tyler and Marla, they were up almost all night in the room next to mine. When Tyler woke up, Marla had disappeared back to the Regent Hotel.

I tell Tyler, Marla Singer doesn't need a lover, she needs a case worker.

Tyler says, "Don't call this *love.*"

Long story short, now Marla's out to ruin another part of my life. Ever since college, I make friends. They get married. I lose friends.

Fine.

Neat, I say.

Tyler asks, is this a problem for me?

I am Joe's Clenching Bowels.

No, I say, it's fine.

Put a gun to my head and paint the wall with my brains.

Just great, I say. Really.

8

MY BOSS SENDS me home because of all the dried blood on my pants, and I am overjoyed.

The hole punched through my cheek doesn't ever heal. I'm going to work, and my punched-out eye sockets are two swollen-up black bagels around the little piss holes I have left to see through. Until today, it really pissed me off that I'd become this totally centered Zen Master and nobody had noticed. Still, I'm doing the little FAX thing. I write little HAIKU things and FAX them around to everyone. When I pass people in the hall at work, I get totally ZEN right in everyone's hostile little FACE.

> Worker bees can leave
> Even drones can fly away
> The queen is their slave

You give up all your worldly possessions and your car and go live in a rented house in the toxic waste part of town where late at night, you can hear Marla and Tyler in his room, calling each other human butt wipe.

Take it, human butt wipe.

Do it, butt wipe.

Choke it down. Keep it down, baby.

Just by contrast, this makes me the calm little center of the world.

Me, with my punched-out eyes and dried blood in big black crusty stains on my pants, I'm saying HELLO to everybody at work. HELLO! Look at me. HELLO! I am so ZEN. This is BLOOD. This is NOTHING. Hello. Everything is nothing, and it's so cool to be ENLIGHTENED. Like me.

Sigh.

Look. Outside the window. A bird.

My boss asked if the blood was my blood.

The bird flies downwind. I'm writing a little haiku in my head.

> Without just one nest
> A bird can call the world home
> Life is your career

I'm counting on my fingers: five, seven, five.

The blood, is it mine?

Yeah, I say. Some of it.

This is a wrong answer.

Like this is a big deal. I have two pair of black trousers. Six white shirts. Six pair of underwear. The bare minimum. I go to fight club. These things happen.

"Go home," my boss says. "Get changed."

I'm starting to wonder if Tyler and Marla are the same person. Except for their humping, every night in Marla's room.

Doing it.

Doing it.

Doing it.

Tyler and Marla are never in the same room. I never see them together.

Still, you never see me and Zsa Zsa Gabor together, and this doesn't mean we're the same person. Tyler just doesn't come out when Marla's around.

So I can wash the pants, Tyler has to show me how to make soap. Tyler's upstairs, and the kitchen is filled with the smell of cloves and burnt hair. Marla's at the kitchen table, burning the inside of her arm with a clove cigarette and calling herself human butt wipe.

"I embrace my own festering diseased corruption," Marla tells the cherry on the end of her cigarette. Marla twists the cigarette into the soft white belly of her arm. "Burn, witch, burn."

Tyler's upstairs in my bedroom, looking at his teeth in my mirror, and says he got me a job as a banquet waiter, part time.

"At the Pressman Hotel, if you can work in the evening," Tyler says. "The job will stoke your class hatred."

Yeah, I say, whatever.

"They make you wear a black bow tie," Tyler says. "All you need to work there is a white shirt and black trousers."

Soap, Tyler. I say, we need soap. We need to make some soap. I need to wash my pants.

I hold Tyler's feet while he does two hundred sit-ups.

"To make soap, first we have to render fat." Tyler is full of useful information.

Except for their humping, Marla and Tyler are never in the same room. If Tyler's around, Marla ignores him. This is familiar ground.

This is exactly how my parents were invisible to each other. Then my father went off to start another franchise.

My father always said, "Get married before the sex gets boring, or you'll never get married."

My mother said, "Never buy anything with a nylon zipper."

My parents never said anything you'd want to embroider on a cushion.

Tyler does one hundred ninety-eight sit-ups. One ninety-nine. Two hundred.

Tyler's wearing a sort of gummy flannel bathrobe and sweatpants. "Get Marla out of the house," Tyler says. "Send Marla to the store for a can of lye. The flake kind of lye. Not the crystal kind. Just get rid of her."

Me, I'm six years old, again, and taking messages back and forth between my estranged parents. I hated this when I was six. I hate it now.

Tyler starts doing leg lifts, and I go downstairs to tell Marla: the flake kind of lye, and I give her a ten-dollar bill and my bus pass. While Marla is still sitting at the kitchen table, I take the clove cigarette from between her fingers. Nice and easy. With a dishcloth, I wipe the rusty spots on Marla's arm, where the burn scabs cracked and started to bleed. Then I wedge each of her feet into a high-heel shoe.

Marla looks down at me doing my Prince Charming routine with her shoes and she says, "I let myself in. I didn't think anyone was home. Your front door doesn't lock."

I don't say anything.

"You know, the condom is the glass slipper of our generation. You slip it on when you meet a stranger. You dance all night, then you throw it away. The condom, I mean. Not the stranger."

I'm not talking to Marla. She can horn in on the support groups and Tyler, but there's no way she can be my friend.

"I've been waiting here all morning for you."

> Flowers bloom and die
> Wind brings butterflies or snow
> A stone won't notice

Marla gets up from the kitchen table, and she's wearing a sleeveless blue-colored dress made of some shiny material. Marla pinches the edge of the skirt and turns it up for me to see little dots of stitching on the inside. She's not wearing any underwear. And she winks.

"I wanted to show you my new dress," Marla says. "It's a bridesmaid dress and it's all hand sewn. Do you like it? The Goodwill thrift sold it for one dollar. Somebody did all these tiny stitches just to make this ugly, ugly dress," Marla says. "Can you believe it?"

The skirt is longer on one side than on the other, and the waist of the dress orbits low around Marla's hips.

Before she leaves for the store, Marla lifts her skirt with her fingertips and sort of dances around me and the kitchen table, her ass flying around inside her skirt. What Marla loves, she says, is all the things that people love intensely and then dump an hour or a day after. The way a Christmas tree is the center of attention, then, after Christmas you see those dead Christmas trees with the tinsel still on them, dumped alongside the highway. You see those trees and think of roadkill animals or sex crime victims wearing their underwear inside out and bound with black electrical tape.

I just want her out of here.

"The Animal Control place is the best place to go," Marla says. "Where all the animals, the little doggies and kitties that people loved and then dumped, even the old animals, dance and jump around for your attention because after three days, they get an overdose shot of sodium phenobarbital and then into the big pet oven.

"The big sleep, 'Valley of the Dogs' style.

"Where even if someone loves you enough to save your life, they still castrate you." Marla looks at me as if I'm the one humping her and says, "I can't win with you, can I?"

Marla goes out the back door singing that creepy "Valley of the Dolls" song.

I just stare at her going.

There's one, two, three moments of silence until all of Marla is gone from the room.

I turn around, and Tyler's appeared.

Tyler says, "Did you get rid of her?"

Not a sound, not a smell, Tyler's just appeared.

"First," Tyler says and jumps from the kitchen doorway to digging in the freezer. "First, we need to render some fat."

About my boss, Tyler tells me, if I'm really angry I should go to the post office and fill out a change-of-address card and have all his mail forwarded to Rugby, North Dakota.

Tyler starts pulling out sandwich bags of frozen white stuff and dropping them in the sink. Me, I'm supposed to put a big pan on the stove and fill it most of the way with water. Too little water, and the fat will darken as it separates into tallow.

"This fat," Tyler says, "it has a lot of salt so the more water, the better."

Put the fat in the water, and get the water boiling.

Tyler squeezes the white mess from each sandwich bag into the water, and then Tyler buries the empty bags all the way at the bottom of the trash.

Tyler says, "Use a little imagination. Remember all that pioneer shit they taught you in Boy Scouts. Remember your high school chemistry."

It's hard to imagine Tyler in Boy Scouts.

Another thing I could do, Tyler tells me, is I could drive to my boss's house some night and hook a hose up to an outdoor spigot. Hook the hose to a hand pump, and I could inject the house plumbing with a charge of industrial dye. Red or blue or green, and wait to see how my boss looks the next day. Or, I could just sit in the bushes and pump the hand pump until the plumbing was superpressurized to 110 psi. This way, when someone goes to flush a toilet, the toilet tank will explode. At 150 psi, if someone turns on the shower, the water pressure will blow off the shower head, strip the threads, *blam,* the shower head turns into a mortar shell.

Tyler only says this to make me feel better. The truth is I like my boss. Besides, I'm enlightened now. You know, only Buddha-style behavior. Spider chrysanthemums. The Diamond Sutra and the Blue Cliff Record. Hari Rama, you know, Krishna, Krishna. You know, Enlightened.

"Sticking feathers up your butt," Tyler says, "does not make you a chicken."

As the fat renders, the tallow will float to the surface of the boiling water.

Oh, I say, so I'm sticking feathers up my butt.

As if Tyler here with cigarette burns marching up his arms is such an evolved soul. Mister and Missus Human Butt Wipe. I calm my face down and turn into one of those Hindu cow people going to slaughter on the airline emergency procedure card.

Turn down the heat under the pan.

I stir the boiling water.

More and more tallow will rise until the water is skinned over with a rainbow mother-of-pearl layer. Use a big spoon to skim the layer off, and set this layer aside.

So, I say, how is Marla?

Tyler says, "At least Marla's trying to hit bottom."

I stir the boiling water.

Keep skimming until no more tallow rises. This is tallow we're skimming off the water. Good clean tallow.

Tyler says I'm nowhere near hitting the bottom, yet. And if I don't fall all the way, I can't be saved. Jesus did it with his crucifixion thing. I shouldn't just abandon money and property and knowledge. This isn't just a weekend retreat. I should run from self-improvement, and I should be running toward disaster. I can't just play it safe anymore.

This isn't a seminar.

"If you lose your nerve before you hit the bottom," Tyler says, "you'll never really succeed."

Only after disaster can we be resurrected.

"It's only after you've lost everything," Tyler says, "that you're free to do anything."

What I'm feeling is premature enlightenment.

"And keep stirring," Tyler says.

When the fat's boiled enough that no more tallow rises, throw out the boiling water. Wash the pot and fill it with clean water.

I ask, am I anywhere near hitting bottom?

"Where you're at, now," Tyler says, "you can't even imagine what the bottom will be like."

Repeat the process with the skimmed tallow. Boil the tallow in the water. Skim and keep skimming. "The fat we're using has a lot of salt in it," Tyler says. "Too much salt and your soap won't get solid." Boil and skim.

Boil and skim.

Marla is back.

The second Marla opens the screen door, Tyler is gone, vanished, run out of the room, disappeared.

Tyler's gone upstairs, or Tyler's gone down to the basement.

Poof.

Marla comes in the back door with a canister of lye flakes.

"At the store, they have one-hundred-percent-recycled toilet paper," Marla says. "The worst job in the whole world must be recycling toilet paper."

I take the canister of lye and put it on the table. I don't say anything.

"Can I stay over, tonight?" Marla says.

I don't answer. I count in my head: five syllables, seven, five.

> A tiger can smile
> A snake will say it loves you
> Lies make us evil

Marla says, "What are you cooking?"

I am Joe's Boiling Point.

I say, go, just go, just get out. Okay? Don't you have a big enough chunk of my life, yet?

Marla grabs my sleeve and holds me in one place for the second it takes to kiss my cheek. "Please call me," she says. "Please. We need to talk."

I say, yeah, yeah, yeah, yeah, yeah.

The moment Marla is out the door, Tyler appears back in the room.

Fast as a magic trick. My parents did this magic act for five years.

I boil and skim while Tyler makes room in the fridge. Steam layers the air and water drips from the kitchen ceiling. The forty-watt bulb hidden in the back of the fridge, something bright I can't see behind the empty ketchup bottles and jars of pickle brine or mayonnaise, some tiny light from inside the fridge edges Tyler's profile bright.

Boil and skim. Boil and skim. Put the skimmed tallow into milk cartons with the tops opened all the way.

With a chair pulled up to the open fridge, Tyler watches the tallow cool. In the heat of the kitchen, clouds of cold fog waterfall out from the bottom of the fridge and pool around Tyler's feet.

As I fill the milk cartons with tallow, Tyler puts them in the fridge.

I go to kneel beside Tyler in front of the fridge, and Tyler takes my hands and shows them to me. The life line. The love line. The mounds of Venus and Mars. The cold fog pooling around us, the dim bright light on our faces.

"I need you to do me another favor," Tyler says.

This is about Marla isn't it?

"Don't ever talk to her about me. Don't talk about me behind my back. Do you promise?" Tyler says.

I promise.

Tyler says, "If you ever mention me to her, you'll never see me again."

I promise.

"Promise?"

I promise.

Tyler says, "Now remember, that was three times that you promised."

A layer of something thick and clear is collecting on top of the tallow in the fridge.

The tallow, I say, it's separating.

"Don't worry," Tyler says. "The clear layer is glycerin. You can mix the glycerin back in when you make soap. Or, you can skim the glycerin off."

Tyler licks his lips, and turns my hands palm-down on his thigh, on the gummy flannel lap of his bathrobe.

"You can mix the glycerin with nitric acid to make nitroglycerin," Tyler says.

I breathe with my mouth open and say, nitroglycerin.

Tyler licks his lips wet and shining and kisses the back of my hand.

"You can mix the nitroglycerin with sodium nitrate and sawdust to make dynamite," Tyler says.

The kiss shines wet on the back of my white hand.

Dynamite, I say, and sit back on my heels.

Tyler pries the lid off the can of lye. "You can blow up bridges," Tyler says.

"You can mix the nitroglycerin with more nitric acid and paraffin and make gelatin explosives," Tyler says.

"You could blow up a building, easy," Tyler says.

Tyler tilts the can of lye an inch above the shining wet kiss on the back of my hand.

"This is a chemical burn," Tyler says, "and it will hurt worse than you've ever been burned. Worse than a hundred cigarettes."

The kiss shines on the back of my hand.

"You'll have a scar," Tyler says.

"With enough soap," Tyler says, "you could blow up the whole world. Now remember your promise."

And Tyler pours the lye.

9

TYLER'S SALIVA DID two jobs. The wet kiss on the back of my hand held the flakes of lye while they burned. That was the first job. The second was lye only burns when you combine it with water. Or saliva.

"This is a chemical burn," Tyler said, "and it will hurt more than you've ever been burned."

You can use lye to open clogged drains.

Close your eyes.

A paste of lye and water can burn through an aluminum pan.

A solution of lye and water will dissolve a wooden spoon.

Combined with water, lye heats to over two hundred degrees, and as it heats it burns into the back of my hand, and Tyler places his fingers of one hand over my fingers, our hands spread on the lap of my bloodstained pants, and Tyler says to pay attention because this is the greatest moment of my life.

"Because everything up to now is a story," Tyler says, "and everything after now is a story."

This is the greatest moment of our life.

The lye clinging in the exact shape of Tyler's kiss is a bonfire or a branding iron or an atomic pile meltdown on my hand at the end of a long, long road I picture miles away from me. Tyler tells me to come back and be with him. My hand is leaving, tiny and on the horizon at the end of the road.

Picture the fire still burning, except now it's beyond the horizon. A sunset.

"Come back to the pain," Tyler says.

This is the kind of guided meditation they use at support groups.

Don't even think of the word *pain*.

Guided meditation works for cancer, it can work for this.

"Look at your hand," Tyler says.

Don't look at your hand.

Don't think of the word *searing* or *flesh* or *tissue* or *charred*.

Don't hear yourself cry.

Guided meditation.

You're in Ireland. Close your eyes.

You're in Ireland the summer after you left college, and you're drinking at a pub near the castle where every day busloads of English and American tourists come to kiss the Blarney stone.

"Don't shut this out," Tyler says. "Soap and human sacrifice go hand in hand."

You leave the pub in a stream of men, walking through the beaded wet car silence of streets where it's just rained. It's night. Until you get to the Blarney-stone castle.

The floors in the castle are rotted away, and you climb the rock stairs with blackness getting deeper and deeper on every side with every step up. Everybody is quiet with the climb and the tradition of this little act of rebellion.

"Listen to me," Tyler says. "Open your eyes.

"In ancient history," Tyler says, "human sacrifices were made on a hill above a river. Thousands of people. Listen to me. The sacrifices were made and the bodies were burned on a pyre.

"You can cry," Tyler says. "You can go to the sink and run water over your hand, but first you have to know that you're stupid and you will die. Look at me.

"Someday," Tyler says, "you will die, and until you know that, you're useless to me."

You're in Ireland.

"You can cry," Tyler says, "but every tear that lands in the lye flakes on your skin will burn a cigarette burn scar."

Guided meditation. You're in Ireland the summer after you left college, and maybe this is where you first wanted anarchy. Years before you met Tyler Durden, before you peed in your first crème anglaise, you learned about little acts of rebellion.

In Ireland.

You're standing on a platform at the top of the stairs in a castle.

"We can use vinegar," Tyler says, "to neutralize the burning, but first you have to give up."

After hundreds of people were sacrificed and burned, Tyler says, a thick white discharge crept from the altar, downhill to the river.

First you have to hit bottom.

You're on a platform in a castle in Ireland with bottomless darkness all around the edge of the platform, and ahead of you, across an arm's length of darkness, is a rock wall.

"Rain," Tyler says, "fell on the burnt pyre year after year, and year after year, people were burned, and the rain seeped through the wood ashes to become a solution of lye, and the lye combined with the melted fat of the sacrifices, and a thick white discharge of soap crept out from the base of the altar and crept downhill toward the river."

And the Irish men around you with their little act of rebellion in the darkness, they walk to the edge of the platform, and stand at the edge of the bottomless darkness and piss.

And the men say, go ahead, piss your fancy American piss rich and yellow with too many vitamins. Rich and expensive and thrown away.

"This is the greatest moment of your life," Tyler says, "and you're off somewhere missing it."

You're in Ireland.

Oh, and you're doing it. Oh, yeah. Yes. And you can smell the ammonia and the daily allowance of B vitamins.

Where the soap fell into the river, Tyler says, after a thousand years of killing people and rain, the ancient people found their clothes got cleaner if they washed at that spot.

I'm pissing on the Blarney stone.

"Geez," Tyler says.

I'm pissing in my black trousers with the dried bloodstains my boss can't stomach.

You're in a rented house on Paper Street.

"This means something," Tyler says.

"This is a sign," Tyler says. Tyler is full of useful information. Cultures without soap, Tyler says, they used their urine and the urine of their dogs to wash their clothes and hair because of the uric acid and ammonia.

There's the smell of vinegar, and the fire on your hand at the end of the long road goes out.

There's the smell of lye scalding the branched shape of your sinuses, and the hospital vomit smell of piss and vinegar.

"It was right to kill all those people," Tyler says.

The back of your hand is swollen red and glossy as a pair of lips in the exact shape of Tyler's kiss. Scattered around the kiss are the cigarette burn spots of somebody crying.

"Open your eyes," Tyler says, and his face is shining with tears. "Congratulations," Tyler says. "You're a step closer to hitting bottom.

"You have to see," Tyler says, "how the first soap was made of heroes."

Think about the animals used in product testing.

Think about the monkeys shot into space.

"Without their death, their pain, without their sacrifice," Tyler says, "we would have nothing."

I STOP THE elevator between floors while Tyler undoes his belt. When the elevator stops, the soup bowls stacked on the buffet cart stop rattling, and steam mushrooms up to the elevator ceiling as Tyler takes the lid off the soup tureen.

Tyler starts to take himself out and says, "Don't look at me, or I can't go."

The soup's a sweet tomato bisque with cilantro and clams. Between the two, nobody will smell anything else we put in.

I say, hurry up, and I look back over my shoulder at Tyler with his last half inch hanging in the soup. This looks in a really funny way like a tall elephant in a waiter's white shirt and bow tie drinking soup through its little trunk.

Tyler says, "I said, 'Don't look.'"

The elevator door in front of me has a little face-sized window that lets me look out into the banquet service corridor. With the elevator stopped between floors, my view is about a cockroach above the green linoleum, and from here at cockroach level the green corridor stretches toward the vanishing point, past half-open doors where titans and their gigantic wives drink barrels of champagne and bellow at each other wearing diamonds bigger than I feel.

Last week, I tell Tyler, when the Empire State Lawyers were here for their Christmas party, I got mine hard and stuck it in all their orange mousses.

Last week, Tyler says, he stopped the elevator and farted on a whole cart of Boccone Dolce for the Junior League tea.

That Tyler knows how a meringue will absorb odor.

At cockroach level, we can hear the captive harpist make music as the titans lift forks of butterflied lamb chop, each bite the size of a whole pig, each mouth a tearing Stonehenge of ivory.

I say, go already.

Tyler says, "I can't."

If the soup gets cold, they'll send it back.

The giants, they'll send something back to the kitchen for no reason at all. They just want to see you run around for their money. A dinner like this, these banquet parties, they know the tip is already included in the bill so they treat you like dirt. We don't really take anything back to the kitchen. Move the Pommes Parisienne and the Asperges Hollandaise around the plate a little, serve it to someone else, and all of a sudden it's fine.

I say, Niagara Falls. The Nile River. In school, we all thought if you put somebody's hand in a bowl of warm water while they slept, they'd wet the bed.

Tyler says, "Oh." Behind me, Tyler says, "Oh, yeah. Oh, I'm doing it. Oh, yeah. Yes."

Past half-open doors in the ballrooms off the service corridor swish gold and black and red skirts as tall as the gold velvet curtain at the old Broadway Theatre. Now and again there are pairs of Cadillac sedans in black leather with shoelaces where the windshields should be. Above the cars move a city of office towers in red cummerbunds.

Not too much, I say.

Tyler and me, we've turned into the guerrilla terrorists of the service industry. Dinner party saboteurs. The hotel caters dinner parties, and when somebody wants the food they get the food and the wine and the china and glassware and the waiters. They get the works, all on one bill. And because they know they can't threaten you with the tip, to them you're just a cockroach.

Tyler, he did a dinner party one time. This was when Tyler turned into a renegade waiter. That first dinner party, Tyler was serving the fish course in this white and glass cloud of a house that seemed to float over the city on steel legs attached to a hillside. Part of the way through the fish course, while Tyler's rinsing plates from the pasta course, the hostess comes in the kitchen holding a scrap of paper that flaps like a flag, her hand is shaking so much. Through her clenched teeth, Madam wants to know did the waiters see any of the guests go down the hallway that leads to the bedroom part of the house? Especially any of the women guests? Or the host?

In the kitchen, it's Tyler and Albert and Len and Jerry rinsing and stacking the plates and a prep cook, Leslie, basting garlic butter on the artichoke hearts stuffed with shrimp and escargot.

"We're not supposed to go in that part of the house," Tyler says.

We come in through the garage. All we're supposed to see is the garage, the kitchen, and the dining room.

The host comes in behind his wife in the kitchen doorway and takes the scrap of paper out of her shaking hand. "This will be alright," he says.

"How can I face those people," Madam says, "unless I know who did this?"

The host puts a flat open hand against the back of her silky white party dress that matches her house and Madam straightens up, her shoulders squared, and is all of a sudden quiet. "They are your guests," he says. "And this party is very important."

This looks in a really funny way like a ventriloquist bringing his dummy to life. Madam looks at her husband, and with a little shove the host takes his wife back into the dining room. The note drops to the floor and the two-way *swish, swish* of the kitchen door sweeps the note against Tyler's feet.

Albert says, "What's it say?"

Len goes out to start clearing the fish course.

Leslie slides the tray of artichoke hearts back into the oven and says, "What's it say, already?"

Tyler looks right at Leslie and says, without even picking up the note, " 'I have passed an amount of urine into at least one of your many elegant fragrances.' "

Albert smiles. "You pissed in her perfume?"

No, Tyler says. He just left the note stuck between the bottles. She's got about a hundred bottles sitting on a mirror counter in her bathroom.

Leslie smiles. "So you didn't, really?"

"No," Tyler says, "but she doesn't know that."

The whole rest of the night in that white and glass dinner party in the sky, Tyler kept clearing plates of cold artichokes, then cold veal with cold Pommes Duchesse, then cold Choufleur à la Polonaise from in front of the hostess, and Tyler kept filling her wine glass about a dozen times. Madam sat watching each of her women guests eat the food, until between clearing the sorbet dishes and serving the apricot gateau, Madam's place at the head of the table was all of a sudden empty.

They were washing up after the guests had left, loading the coolers and the china back into the hotel van, when the host came in the kitchen and asked, would Albert please come help him with something heavy?

Leslie says, maybe Tyler went too far.

Loud and fast, Tyler says how they kill whales, Tyler says, to make that perfume that costs more than gold per ounce. Most people have never seen a whale. Leslie has two kids in an apartment next to the freeway and Madam hostess has more bucks than we'll make in a year in bottles on her bathroom counter.

Albert comes back from helping the host and dials 9-1-1 on the phone. Albert puts a hand over the mouth part and says, man, Tyler shouldn't have left that note.

Tyler says, "So, tell the banquet manager. Get me fired. I'm not married to this chickenshit job."

Everybody looks at their feet.

"Getting fired," Tyler says, "is the best thing that could happen to any of us. That way, we'd quit treading water and do something with our lives."

Albert says into the phone that we need an ambulance and the address. Waiting on the line, Albert says the hostess is a real mess right now. Albert had to pick her up from next to the toilet. The host couldn't pick her up because Madam says he's the one who peed in her perfume bottles, and she says he's trying to drive her crazy by having an affair with one of the women guests, tonight, and she's tired, tired of all the people they call their friends.

The host can't pick her up because Madam's fallen down behind the toilet in her white dress and she's waving around half a broken perfume bottle. Madam says she'll cut his throat, he even tries to touch her.

Tyler says, "Cool."

And Albert stinks. Leslie says, "Albert, honey, you stink."

There's no way you could come out of that bathroom not stinking,

Albert says. Every bottle of perfume is broken on the floor and the toilet is piled full of the other bottles. They look like ice, Albert says, like at the fanciest hotel parties where we have to fill the urinals with crushed ice. The bathroom stinks and the floor is gritty with slivers of ice that won't melt, and when Albert helps Madam to her feet, her white dress wet with yellow stains, Madam swings the broken bottle at the host, slips in the perfume and broken glass, and lands on her palms.

She's crying and bleeding, curled against the toilet. Oh, and it stings, she says. "Oh, Walter, it stings. It's stinging," Madam says.

The perfume, all those dead whales in the cuts in her hands, it stings.

The host pulls Madam to her feet against him, Madam holding her hands up as if she were praying but with her hands an inch apart and blood running down the palms, down the wrists, across a diamond bracelet, and to her elbows where it drips.

And the host, he says, "It will be alright, Nina."

"My hands, Walter," Madam says.

"It will be alright."

Madam says, "Who would do this to me? Who could hate me this much?"

The host says, to Albert, "Would you call an ambulance?"

That was Tyler's first mission as a service industry terrorist. Guerrilla waiter. Minimum-wage despoiler. Tyler's been doing this for years, but he says everything is more fun as a shared activity.

At the end of Albert's story, Tyler smiles and says, "Cool."

Back in the hotel, right now, in the elevator stopped between the kitchen and the banquet floors, I tell Tyler how I sneezed on the trout in aspic for the dermatologist convention and three people told me it was too salty and one person said it was delicious.

Tyler shakes himself off over the soup tureen and says he's run dry.

This is easier with cold soup, vichyssoise, or when the chefs make a really fresh gazpacho. This is impossible with that onion soup that has a crust of melted cheese on it in ramekins. If I ever ate here, that's what I'd order.

We were running out of ideas, Tyler and me. Doing stuff to the food got to be boring, almost part of the job description. Then I hear one of the doctors, lawyers, whatever, say how a hepatitis bug can live on stainless steel for six months. You have to wonder how long this bug can live on Rum Custard Charlotte Russe.

Or Salmon Timbale.

I asked the doctor where could we get our hands on some of these hepatitis bugs, and he's drunk enough to laugh.

Everything goes to the medical waste dump, he says.

And he laughs.

Everything.

The medical waste dump sounds like hitting bottom.

One hand on the elevator control, I ask Tyler if he's ready. The scar on the back of my hand is swollen red and glossy as a pair of lips in the exact shape of Tyler's kiss.

"One second," Tyler says.

The tomato soup must still be hot because the crooked thing Tyler tucks back in his pants is boiled pink as a jumbo prawn.

11

IN SOUTH AMERICA, Land of Enchantment, we could be wading in a river where tiny fish will swim up Tyler's urethra. The fish have barbed spines that flare out and back so once they're up Tyler, the fish set up housekeeping and get ready to lay their eggs. In so many ways, how we spent Saturday night could be worse.

"It could've been worse," Tyler says, "what we did with Marla's mother."

I say, shut up.

Tyler says, the French government could've taken us to an underground complex outside of Paris where not even surgeons but semi-skilled technicians would razor our eyelids off as part of toxicity testing an aerosol tanning spray.

"This stuff happens," Tyler says. "Read the newspaper."

What's worse is I knew what Tyler had been up to with Marla's mother, but for the first time since I've known him, Tyler had some real play money. Tyler was making real bucks. Nordstrom's called and left an order for two hundred bars of Tyler's brown sugar facial soap before Christmas. At twenty bucks a bar, suggested retail price, we had money to go out on Saturday night. Money to fix the leak in the gas line. Go dancing. Without money to worry about, maybe I could quit my job.

Tyler calls himself the Paper Street Soap Company. People are saying it's the best soap ever.

"What would've been worse," Tyler says, "is if you had accidentally eaten Marla's mother."

Through a mouthful of Kung Pao Chicken, I say to just shut the hell up.

Where we are this Saturday night is the front seat of a 1968 Impala sitting on two flats in the front row of a used-car lot. Tyler and me, we're talking, drinking beer out of cans, and the front seat of this Impala is bigger than most people's sofas. The car lots up and down this part of the boulevard, in the industry they call these lots the Pot Lots where the cars all cost around two hundred dollars and during the day, the gypsy guys who run these lots stand around in their plywood offices smoking long, thin cigars.

The cars are the beater first cars kids drive in high school: Gremlins and Pacers, Mavericks and Hornets, Pintos, International Harvester pickup trucks, lowered Camaros and Dusters and Impalas. Cars that people loved and then dumped. Animals at the pound. Bridesmaid dresses at the Goodwill. With dents and gray or red or black primer quarter panels and rocker panels and lumps of body putty that nobody ever got around to sanding. Plastic wood and plastic leather and plastic chrome interiors. At night, the gypsy guys don't even lock the car doors.

The headlights on the boulevard go by behind the price painted on the Impala-big wraparound Cinemascope windshield. See the U.S.A. The price is ninety-eight dollars. From the inside, this looks like eighty-nine cents. Zero, zero, decimal point, eight, nine. America is asking you to call.

Most of the cars here are about a hundred dollars, and all the cars have an "AS IS" sales agreement hanging in the driver's window.

We chose the Impala because if we have to sleep in a car on Saturday night, this car has the biggest seats.

We're eating Chinese because we can't go home. It was either sleep here, or stay up all night at an after-hours dance club. We don't go to dance clubs. Tyler says the music is so loud, especially the base tracks, that it screws with his biorhythm. The last time we went out, Tyler said the loud music made him constipated. This, and the club is too loud to talk, so after a couple of drinks, everyone feels like the center of attention but completely cut off from participating with anyone else.

You're the corpse in an English murder mystery.

We're sleeping in a car tonight because Marla came to the house and threatened to call the police and have me arrested for cooking her mother, and then Marla slammed around the house, screaming that I was a ghoul and a cannibal and she went kicking through the piles of *Reader's Digest* and *National Geographic,* and then I left her there. In a nutshell.

After her accidental on-purpose suicide with Xanax at the Regent Hotel, I can't imagine Marla calling the police, but Tyler thought it would be good to sleep out, tonight. Just in case.

Just in case Marla burns the house down.

Just in case Marla goes out and finds a gun.

Just in case Marla is still in the house.

Just in case.

I try to get centered:

Watching white moon face
The stars never feel anger
Blah, blah, blah, the end

Here, with the cars going by on the boulevard and a beer in my hand in the Impala with its cold, hard Bakelite steering wheel maybe three feet in diameter and the cracked vinyl seat pinching my ass through my jeans, Tyler says, "One more time. Tell me exactly what happened."

For weeks, I ignored what Tyler had been up to. One time, I went with Tyler to the Western Union office and watched as he sent Marla's mother a telegram.

HIDEOUSLY WRINKLED (stop) PLEASE HELP ME! (end)

Tyler had showed the clerk Marla's library card and signed Marla's name to the telegram order, and yelled, yes, Marla can be a guy's name sometimes, and the clerk could just mind his own business.

When we were leaving the Western Union, Tyler said if I loved him, I'd trust him. This wasn't something I needed to know about, Tyler told me and he took me to Garbonzo's for hummus.

What really scared me wasn't the telegram as much as it was eating out with Tyler. Never, no, never had Tyler ever paid cash for anything. For clothes, Tyler goes to gyms and hotels and claims clothing out of the lost and found. This is better than Marla, who goes to Laundromats to steal jeans out of the dryers and sell them at twelve dollars a pair to those places that buy used jeans. Tyler never ate in restaurants, and Marla wasn't wrinkled.

For no apparent reason, Tyler sent Marla's mother a fifteen-pound box of chocolates.

Another way this Saturday night could be worse, Tyler tells me in the Impala, is the brown recluse spider. When it bites you, it injects not just a venom but a digestive enzyme or acid that dissolves the tissue around the bite, literally melting your arm or your leg or your face.

Tyler was hiding out tonight when this all started. Marla showed up at the house. Without even knocking, Marla leans inside the front door and shouts, "Knock, knock."

I'm reading *Reader's Digest* in the kitchen. I am totally nonplussed.

Marla yells, "Tyler. Can I come in? Are you home?"

I yell, Tyler's not home.

Marla yells, "Don't be mean."

By now, I'm at the front door. Marla's standing in the foyer with a Federal Express overnight package, and says, "I needed to put something in your freezer."

I dog her heels on the way to the kitchen, saying, no.

No.

No.

No.

She is not going to start keeping her junk in this house.

"But Pumpkin," Marla says, "I don't have a freezer at the hotel, and you said I could."

No, I did not. The last thing I want is Marla moving in, one piece of crap at a time.

Marla has her Federal Express package ripped open on the kitchen table, and she lifts something white out of the Styrofoam packing peanuts and shakes this white thing in my face. "This is not crap," she says. "This is my mother you're talking about so just fuck off."

What Marla lifts out of the package, it's one of those sandwich bags of white stuff that Tyler rendered for tallow to make soap.

"Things would've been worse," Tyler says, "if you'd accidentally eaten what was in one of those sandwich bags. If you'd got up in the middle of the night sometime, and squeezed out the white goo and added California onion soup mix and eaten it as a dip with potato chips. Or broccoli."

More than anything in the world right then, while Marla and I were standing in the kitchen, I didn't want Marla to open the freezer.

I asked, what was she going to do with the white stuff?

"Paris lips," Marla said. "As you get older, your lips pull inside your mouth. I'm saving for a collagen lip injection. I have almost thirty pounds of collagen in your freezer."

I asked, how big of lips did she want?

Marla said it was the operation itself that scared her.

The stuff in the Federal Express package, I tell Tyler in the Impala, that was the same stuff we made soap out of. Ever since silicone turned out to be dangerous, collagen has become the hot item to have injected to smooth out wrinkles or to puff up thin lips or weak chins. The way Marla had explained it, most collagen you get cheap is from cow fat that's been sterilized and processed, but that kind of cheap collagen doesn't last very long in your body. Wherever you get it injected, say in your lips, your body rejects it and starts to poop it out. Six months later, you have thin lips, again.

The best kind of collagen, Marla said, is your own fat, sucked out of your thighs, processed and cleaned and injected back into your lips. Or wherever. This kind of collagen will last.

This stuff in the fridge at home, it was Marla's collagen trust fund. Whenever her mom grew any extra fat, she had it sucked out and packaged. Marla says the process is called *gleaning*. If Marla's mom doesn't need the collagen herself, she sends the packets to Marla. Marla never has any fat of her own, and her mom figures that familial collagen would be better than Marla ever having to use the cheap cow kind.

Streetlight along the boulevard comes through the sales agreement in the window and prints "AS IS" on Tyler's cheek.

"Spiders," Tyler says, "could lay their eggs and larva could tunnel under your skin. That's how bad your life can get."

Right now, my Almond Chicken in its warm, creamy sauce tastes like something sucked out of Marla's mother's thighs.

It was right then, standing in the kitchen with Marla, that I knew what Tyler had done.

HIDEOUSLY WRINKLED.

And I knew why he sent candy to Marla's mother.

PLEASE HELP.

I say, Marla, you don't want to look in the freezer.

Marla says, "Do what?"

"We never eat red meat," Tyler tells me in the Impala, and he can't use chicken fat or the soap won't harden into a bar. "The stuff," Tyler says, "is making us a fortune. We paid the rent with that collagen."

I say, you should've told Marla. Now she thinks I did it.

"Saponification," Tyler says, "is the chemical reaction you need to make good soap. Chicken fat won't work or any fat with too much salt.

"Listen," Tyler says. "We have a big order to fill. What we'll do is send Marla's mom some chocolates and probably some fruitcakes."

I don't think that will work, anymore.

Long story short, Marla looked in the freezer. Okay, there was a little scuffle, first. I try to stop her, and the bag she's holding gets dropped and breaks open on the linoleum and we both slip in the greasy white mess and come up gagging. I have Marla around the waist from behind, her black hair whipping my face, her arms pinned to her sides, and I'm saying over and over, it wasn't me. It wasn't me.

I didn't do it.

"My mother! You're spilling her all over!"

We needed to make soap, I say with my face pressed up behind her ear. We needed to wash my pants, to pay the rent, to fix the leak in the gas line. It wasn't me.

It was Tyler.

Marla screams, "What are you talking about?" and twists out of her skirt. I'm scrambling to get up off the greased floor with an armful of Marla's India cotton print skirt, and Marla in her panties and wedgie heels and peasant blouse throws open the freezer part of the fridge, and inside there's no collagen trust fund.

There's two old flashlight batteries, but that's all.

"Where is she?"

I'm already crawling backwards, my hands slipping, my shoes slipping on the linoleum, and my ass wiping a clean path across the dirty floor away from Marla and the fridge. I hold up the skirt so I don't have to see Marla's face when I tell her.

The truth.

We made soap out of it. Her. Marla's mother.

"Soap?"

Soap. You boil fat. You mix it with lye. You get soap.

When Marla screams, I throw the skirt in her face and run. I slip. I run.

Around and around the first floor, Marla runs after me, skidding on the corners, pushing off against the window casings for momentum. Slipping.

Leaving filthy handprints of grease and floor dirt among the wallpaper flowers. Falling and sliding into the wainscoting, getting back up, running.

Marla screaming, "You boiled my mother!"

Tyler boiled her mother.

Marla screaming, always one swipe of her fingernails behind me.

Tyler boiled her mother.

"You boiled my mother!"

The front door was still open.

And then I was out the front door with Marla screaming in the doorway behind me. My feet didn't slip against the concrete sidewalk, and I just kept running. Until I found Tyler or until Tyler found me, and I told him what happened.

With one beer each, Tyler and I spread out on the front and back seats with me in the front seat. Even now, Marla's probably still in the house, throwing magazines against the walls and screaming how I'm a prick and a monster two-faced capitalist suck-ass bastard. The miles of night between Marla and me offer insects and melanomas and flesh-eating viruses. Where I'm at isn't so bad.

"When a man is hit by lightning," Tyler says, "his head burns down to a smoldering baseball and his zipper welds itself shut."

I say, did we hit bottom, tonight?

Tyler lies back and asks, "If Marilyn Monroe was alive right now, what would she be doing?"

I say, goodnight.

The headliner hangs down in shreds from the ceiling, and Tyler says, "Clawing at the lid of her coffin."

12

MY BOSS STANDS too close to my desk with his little smile, his lips together and stretched thin, his crotch at my elbow. I look up from writing the cover letter for a recall campaign. These letters always begin the same way:

"This notice is sent to you in accordance with the requirements of the National Motor Vehicle Safety Act. We have determined that a defect exists . . ."

This week I ran the liability formula, and for once A times B times C equaled more than the cost of a recall.

This week, it's the little plastic clip that holds the rubber blade on your windshield wipers. A throwaway item. Only two hundred vehicles affected. Next to nothing for the labor cost.

Last week was more typical. Last week the issue was some leather cured with a known teratogenic substance, synthetic Nirret or something just as illegal that's still used in third world tanning. Something so strong that it could cause birth defects in the fetus of any pregnant woman who comes across it. Last week, nobody called the Department of Transportation. Nobody initiated a recall.

New leather multiplied by labor cost multiplied by administration cost would equal more than our first-quarter profits. If anyone ever discovers our mistake, we can still pay off a lot of grieving families before we come close to the cost of retrofitting sixty-five hundred leather interiors.

But this week, we're doing a recall campaign. And this week the insomnia is back. Insomnia, and now the whole world figures to stop by and take a dump on my grave.

My boss is wearing his gray tie so today must be a Tuesday.

My boss brings a sheet of paper to my desk and asks if I'm looking for something. This paper was left in the copy machine, he says, and begins to read:

"The first rule of fight club is you don't talk about fight club."

His eyes go side to side across the paper, and he giggles.

"The second rule of fight club is you don't talk about fight club."

I hear Tyler's words come out of my boss, Mister Boss with his midlife spread and family photo on his desk and his dreams about early retirement and winters spent at a trailer-park hookup in some Arizona desert. My boss, with his extra-starched shirts and standing appointment for a haircut every Tuesday after lunch, he looks at me, and he says:

"I hope this isn't yours."

I am Joe's Blood-Boiling Rage.

Tyler asked me to type up the fight club rules and make him ten copies. Not nine, not eleven. Tyler says, ten. Still, I have the insomnia, and can't remember sleeping since three nights ago. This must be the original I typed. I made ten copies, and forgot the original. The paparazzi flash of the copy machine in my face. The insomnia distance of everything, a copy of a copy of a copy. You can't touch anything, and nothing can touch you.

My boss reads:

"The third rule of fight club is two men per fight."

Neither of us blinks.

My boss reads:

"One fight at a time."

I haven't slept in three days unless I'm sleeping now. My boss shakes the paper under my nose. What about it, he says. Is this some little game I'm playing on company time? I'm paid for my full attention, not to waste time with little war games. And I'm not paid to abuse the copy machines.

What about it? He shakes the paper under my nose. What do I think, he asks, what should he do with an employee who spends company time in some little fantasy world. If I was in his shoes, what would I do?

What would I do?

The hole in my cheek, the blue-black swelling around my eyes, and the swollen red scar of Tyler's kiss on the back of my hand, a copy of a copy of a copy.

Speculation.

Why does Tyler want ten copies of the fight club rules?

Hindu cow.

What I would do, I say, is I'd be very careful who I talked to about this paper.

I say, it sounds like some dangerous psychotic killer wrote this, and this buttoned-down schizophrenic could probably go over the edge at any moment in the working day and stalk from office to office with an Armalite AR-180 carbine gas-operated semiautomatic.

My boss just looks at me.

The guy, I say, is probably at home every night with a little rattail file, filing a cross into the tip of every one of his rounds. This way, when he shows up to work one morning and pumps a round into his nagging, ineffectual, petty, whining, butt-sucking, candy-ass boss, that one round will split along the filed grooves and spread open the way a dumdum bullet flowers inside you to blow a bushel load of your stinking guts out through your spine. Picture your gut chakra opening in a slow-motion explosion of sausage-casing small intestine.

My boss takes the paper out from under my nose.

Go ahead, I say, read some more.

No really, I say, it sounds fascinating. The work of a totally diseased mind.

And I smile. The little butthole-looking edges of the hole in my cheek are the same blue-black as a dog's gums. The skin stretched tight across the swelling around my eyes feels varnished.

My boss just looks at me.

Let me help you, I say.

I say, the fourth rule of fight club is one fight at a time.

My boss looks at the rules and then looks at me.

I say, the fifth rule is no shoes, no shirts in the fight.

My boss looks at the rules and looks at me.

Maybe, I say, this totally diseased fuck would use an Eagle Apache carbine because an Apache takes a thirty-shot mag and only weighs nine pounds. The Armalite only takes a five-round magazine. With thirty shots, our totally fucked hero could go the length of mahogany row and take out every vice-president with a cartridge left over for each director.

Tyler's words coming out of my mouth. I used to be such a nice person.

I just look at my boss. My boss has blue, blue, pale cornflower blue eyes.

The J and R 68 semiautomatic carbine also takes a thirty-shot mag, and it only weighs seven pounds.

My boss just looks at me.

It's scary, I say. This is probably somebody he's known for years. Probably this guy knows all about him, where he lives, and where his wife works and his kids go to school.

This is exhausting, and all of a sudden very, very boring.

And why does Tyler need ten copies of the fight club rules?

What I don't have to say is I know about the leather interiors that cause birth defects. I know about the counterfeit brake linings that looked good enough to pass the purchasing agent, but fail after two thousand miles.

I know about the air-conditioning rheostat that gets so hot it sets fire to the maps in your glove compartment. I know how many people burn alive because of fuel-injector flashback. I've seen people's legs cut off at the knee when turbochargers start exploding and send their vanes through the firewall and into the passenger compartment. I've been out in the field and seen the burned-up cars and seen the reports where CAUSE OF FAILURE is recorded as "unknown."

No, I say, the paper's not mine. I take the paper between two fingers and jerk it out of his hand. The edge must slice his thumb because his hand flies to his mouth, and he's sucking hard, eyes wide open. I crumble the paper into a ball and toss it into the trash can next to my desk.

Maybe, I say, you shouldn't be bringing me every little piece of trash you pick up.

Sunday night, I go to Remaining Men Together and the basement of Trinity Episcopal is almost empty. Just Big Bob, and I come dragging in with every muscle bruised inside and out, but my heart's still racing and my thoughts are a tornado in my head. This is insomnia. All night, your thoughts are on the air.

All night long, you're thinking: Am I asleep? Have I slept?

Insult to injury, Big Bob's arms come out of his T-shirt sleeves quilted with muscle and so hard they shine. Big Bob smiles, he's so happy to see me.

He thought I was dead.

Yeah, I say, me too.

"Well," Big Bob says, "I've got good news."

Where is everybody?

"That's the good news," Big Bob says. "The group's disbanded. I only come down here to tell any guys who might show up."

I collapse with my eyes closed on one of the plaid thrift store couches.

"The good news," Big Bob says, "is there's a new group, but the first rule about this new group is you aren't supposed to talk about it."

Oh.

Big Bob says, "And the second rule is you're not supposed to talk about it."

Oh, shit. I open my eyes.

Fuck.

"The group's called fight club," Big Bob says, "and it meets every Friday night in a closed garage across town. On Thursday nights, there's another fight club that meets at a garage closer by."

I don't know either of these places.

"The first rule about fight club," Big Bob says, "is you don't talk about fight club."

Wednesday, Thursday, and Friday night, Tyler is a movie projectionist. I saw his pay stub last week.

"The second rule about fight club," Big Bob says, "is you don't talk about fight club."

Saturday night, Tyler goes to fight club with me.

"Only two men per fight."

Sunday morning, we come home beat up and sleep all afternoon.

"Only one fight at a time," Big Bob says.

Sunday and Monday night, Tyler's waiting tables.

"You fight without shirts or shoes."

Tuesday night, Tyler's at home making soap, wrapping it in tissue paper, shipping it out. The Paper Street Soap Company.

"The fights," Big Bob says, "go on as long as they have to. Those are the rules invented by the guy who invented fight club."

Big Bob asks, "Do you know him?"

"I've never seen him, myself," Big Bob says, "but the guy's name is Tyler Durden."

The Paper Street Soap Company.

Do I know him.

I dunno, I say.

Maybe.

13

W H E N   I   G E T to the Regent Hotel, Marla's in the lobby wearing a bathrobe. Marla called me at work and asked, would I skip the gym and the library or the laundry or whatever I had planned after work and come see her, instead.

This is why Marla called, because she hates me.

She doesn't say a thing about her collagen trust fund.

What Marla says is, would I do her a favor? Marla was lying in bed this afternoon. Marla lives on the meals that Meals on Wheels delivers for her neighbors who are dead; Marla accepts the meals and says they're asleep. Long story short, this afternoon Marla was just lying in bed, waiting for the Meals on Wheels delivery between noon and two. Marla hasn't had health insurance for a couple years so she's stopped looking, but this morning she looks and there seemed to be a lump and the nodes under her arm near the lump were hard and tender at the same time and she couldn't tell anyone she loves because she doesn't want to scare them and she can't afford to see a doctor if this is nothing, but she needed to talk to someone and someone else needed to look.

The color of Marla's brown eyes is like an animal that's been heated in a furnace and dropped into cold water. They call that vulcanized or galvanized or tempered.

Marla says she'll forgive the collagen thing if I'll help her look.

I figure she doesn't call Tyler because she doesn't want to scare him. I'm neutral in her book, I owe her.

We go upstairs to her room, and Marla tells me how in the wild you don't see old animals because as soon as they age, animals die. If they get sick or slow down, something stronger kills them. Animals aren't meant to get old.

Marla lies down on her bed and undoes the tie on her bathrobe, and says our culture has made death something wrong. Old animals should be an unnatural exception.

Freaks.

Marla's cold and sweating while I tell her how in college I had a wart once. On my penis, only I say, dick. I went to the medical school to have it removed. The wart. Afterwards, I told my father. This was years after, and my dad laughed and told me I was a fool because warts like that are nature's French tickler. Women love them and God was doing me a favor.

Kneeling next to Marla's bed with my hands still cold from outside, feeling Marla's cold skin a little at a time, rubbing a little of Marla between my fingers every inch, Marla says those warts that are God's French ticklers give women cervical cancer.

So I was sitting on the paper belt in an examining room at the medical school while a medical student sprays a canister of liquid nitrogen on my dick and eight medical students watched. This is where you end up if you don't have medical insurance. Only they don't call it a dick, they called it a penis, and whatever you call it, spray it with liquid nitrogen and you might as well burn it with lye, it hurts so bad.

Marla laughs at this until she sees my fingers have stopped. Like maybe I've found something.

Marla stops breathing and her stomach goes like a drum, and her heart is like a fist pounding from inside the tight skin of a drum. But no, I stopped because I'm talking, and I stopped because, for a minute, neither of us was in Marla's bedroom. We were in the medical school years ago, sitting on the sticky paper with my dick on fire with liquid nitrogen when one of the medical students saw my bare feet and left the room fast in two big steps. The student came back in behind three real doctors, and the doctors elbowed the man with the canister of liquid nitrogen to one side.

A real doctor grabbed my bare right foot and hefted it into the face of the other real doctors. The three turned it and poked it and took Polaroid pictures of the foot, and it was as if the rest of the person, half dressed with God's gift half frozen, didn't exist. Only the foot, and the rest of the medical students pressed in to see.

"How long," a doctor asked, "have you had this red blotch on your foot?"

The doctor meant my birthmark. On my right foot is a birthmark that my father jokes looks like a dark red Australia with a little New Zealand right next to it. This is what I told them and it let all the air out of everything. My dick was thawing out. Everyone except the student with the nitrogen left, and there was the sense that he would've left too, he was so disappointed he never met my eyes as he took the head of my dick and stretched it toward himself. The canister jetted a tiny spray on what was left of the wart. The feeling, you could close your eyes and imagine your dick is a hundred miles long, and it would still hurt.

Marla looks down at my hand and the scar from Tyler's kiss.

I said to the medical student, you must not see a lot of birthmarks around here.

It's not that. The student said everyone thought the birthmark was cancer. There was this new kind of cancer that was getting young men. They wake up with a red spot on their feet or ankles. The spots don't go away, they spread until they cover you and then you die.

The student said, the doctors and everyone were so excited because they thought you had this new cancer. Very few people had it, yet, but it was spreading.

This was years and years ago.

Cancer will be like that, I tell Marla. There will be mistakes, and maybe the point is not to forget the rest of yourself if one little part might go bad.

Marla says, *"Might."*

The student with the nitrogen finished up and told me the wart would drop off after a few days. On the sticky paper next to my bare ass was a Polaroid picture of my foot that no one wanted. I said, can I have the picture?

I still have the picture in my room stuck in the corner of a mirror in the frame. I comb my hair in the mirror before work every morning and think how I once had cancer for ten minutes, worse than cancer.

I tell Marla that this Thanksgiving was the first year when my grandfather and I did not go ice skating even though the ice was almost six inches thick. My grandmother always has these little round bandages on her forehead or her arms where moles she's had her whole life didn't look right. They spread out with fringed edges or the moles turned from brown to blue or black.

When my grandmother got out of the hospital the last time, my grandfather was carrying her suitcase and it was so heavy he complained that he felt lopsided. My French-Canadian grandmother was so modest that she never wore a swimming suit in public and she always ran water in the sink to mask any sound she might make in the bathroom. Coming out of Our Lady of Lourdes Hospital after a partial mastectomy, she says: *"You* feel lopsided?"

For my grandfather, that sums up the whole story, my grandmother, cancer, their marriage, your life. He laughs every time he tells that story.

Marla isn't laughing. I want to make her laugh, to warm her up. To make her forgive me for the collagen, I want to tell Marla there's nothing for me to find. If she found anything this morning, it was a mistake. A birthmark.

Marla has the scar from Tyler's kiss on the back of her hand.

I want to make Marla laugh so I don't tell her about the last time I hugged Chloe, Chloe without hair, a skeleton dipped in yellow wax with a silk scarf tied around her bald head. I hugged Chloe one last time before she disappeared forever. I told her she looked like a pirate, and she laughed. Me, when I go to the beach, I always sit with my right foot tucked under me. Australia and New Zealand, or I keep it buried in the sand. My fear is that people will see my foot and I'll start to die in their minds. The cancer I don't have is everywhere now. I don't tell Marla that.

There are a lot of things we don't want to know about the people we love.

To warm her up, to make her laugh, I tell Marla about the woman in Dear Abby who married a handsome successful mortician and on their wedding night, he made her soak in a tub of ice water until her skin was freezing to the touch, and then he made her lie in bed completely still while he had intercourse with her cold inert body.

The funny thing is this woman had done this as a newlywed, and gone on to do it for the next ten years of marriage and now she was writing to Dear Abby to ask if Abby thought it meant something.

14

THIS IS WHY I loved the support groups so much, if people thought you were dying, they gave you their full attention.

If this might be the last time they saw you, they really saw you. Everything else about their checkbook balance and radio songs and messy hair went out the window.

You had their full attention.

People listened instead of just waiting for their turn to speak.

And when they spoke, they weren't telling you a story. When the two of you talked, you were building something, and afterward you were both different than before.

Marla had started going to the support groups after she found the first lump.

The morning after we found her second lump, Marla hopped into the kitchen with both legs in one leg of her pantyhose and said, "Look, I'm a mermaid."

Marla said, "This isn't like when guys sit backward on the toilet and pretend it's a motorcycle. This is a genuine accident."

Just before Marla and I met at Remaining Men Together, there was the first lump, and now there was a second lump.

What you have to know is that Marla is still alive. Marla's philosophy of life, she told me, is that she can die at any moment. The tragedy of her life is that she doesn't.

When Marla found the first lump, she went to a clinic where slumped scarecrow mothers sat in plastic chairs on three sides of the waiting room with limp doll children balled in their laps or lying at their feet. The children were sunken and dark around their eyes the way oranges or bananas go bad and collapse, and the mothers scratched at mats of dandruff from scalp yeast infections out of control. The way the teeth in the clinic looked huge in everyone's thin face, you saw how teeth are just shards of bone that come through your skin to grind things up.

This is where you end up if you don't have health insurance.

Before anyone knew any better, a lot of gay guys had wanted children, and now the children are sick and the mothers are dying and the fathers are dead, and sitting in the hospital vomit smell of piss and vinegar while a nurse asks each mother how long she's been sick and how much weight she's lost and if her child has any living parent or guardian, Marla decides, no.

If she was going to die, Marla didn't want to know about it.

Marla walked around the corner from the clinic to City Laundry and stole all the jeans out of the dryers, then walked to a dealer who gave her fifteen bucks a pair. Then Marla bought herself some really good pantyhose, the kind that don't run.

"Even the good kind that don't run," Marla says, "they snag."

Nothing is static. Everything is falling apart.

Marla started going to the support groups since it was easier to be around other human butt wipe. Everyone has something wrong. And for a while, her heart just sort of flatlined.

Marla started a job doing prepaid funeral plans for a mortuary where sometimes great fat men, but usually fat women, would come out of the mortuary showroom carrying a crematory urn the size of an egg cup, and Marla would sit there at her desk in the foyer with her dark hair tied down and her snagged pantyhose and breast lump and doom, and say, "Madam, don't flatter yourself. We couldn't get even your burned-up head into that tiny thing. Go back and get an urn the size of a bowling ball."

Marla's heart looked the way my face was. The crap and the trash of the world. Post-consumer human butt wipe that no one would ever go to the trouble to recycle.

Between the support groups and the clinic, Marla told me, she had met a lot of people who were dead. These people were dead and on the other side, and at night they called on the telephone. Marla would go to bars and hear the bartender calling her name, and when she took the call the line was dead.

At the time, she thought this was hitting bottom.

"When you're twenty-four," Marla says, "you have no idea how far you can really fall, but I was a fast learner."

The first time Marla filled a crematory urn, she didn't wear a face mask, and later she blew her nose and there in the tissue was a black mess of Mr. Whoever.

In the house on Paper Street, if the phone rang only once and you picked it up and the line was dead, you knew it was someone trying to reach Marla. This happened more than you might think.

In the house on Paper Street, a police detective started calling about my condominium explosion, and Tyler stood with his chest against my shoulder, whispering into my ear while I held the phone to the other ear, and the detective asked if I knew anyone who could make homemade dynamite.

"Disaster is a natural part of my evolution," Tyler whispered, "toward tragedy and dissolution."

I told the detective that it was the refrigerator that blew up my condo.

"I'm breaking my attachment to physical power and possessions," Tyler whispered, "because only through destroying myself can I discover the greater power of my spirit."

The dynamite, the detective said, there were impurities, a residue of ammonium oxalate and potassium perchloride that might mean the bomb was homemade, and the dead bolt on the front door was shattered.

I said I was in Washington, D.C., that night.

The detective on the phone explained how someone had sprayed a canister of Freon into the dead-bolt lock and then tapped the lock with a cold chisel to shatter the cylinder. This is the way criminals are stealing bicycles.

"The liberator who destroys my property," Tyler said, "is fighting to save my spirit. The teacher who clears all possessions from my path will set me free."

The detective said whoever set the homemade dynamite could've turned on the gas and blown out the pilot lights on the stove days before the explosion took place. The gas was just the trigger. It would take days for the gas to fill the condo before it reached the compressor at the base of the refrigerator and the compressor's electric motor set off the explosion.

"Tell him," Tyler whispered. "Yes, you did it. You blew it all up. That's what he wants to hear."

I tell the detective, no, I did not leave the gas on and then leave town. I loved my life. I loved that condo. I loved every stick of furniture. That was my whole life. Everything, the lamps, the chairs, the rugs were me. The dishes in the cabinets were me. The plants were me. The television was me. It was me that blew up. Couldn't he see that?

The detective said not to leave town.

15

MISTER HIS HONOR, mister chapter president of the local chapter of the national united projectionist and independent theater operators union just sat.

Under and behind and inside everything the man took for granted, something horrible had been growing.

Nothing is static.

Everything is falling apart.

I know this because Tyler knows this.

For three years Tyler had been doing film buildup and breakdown for a chain of movie houses. A movie travels in six or seven small reels packed in a metal case. Tyler's job was to splice the small reels together into single five-foot reels that self-threading and rewinding projectors could handle. After three years, seven theaters, at least three screens per theater, new shows every week, Tyler had handled hundreds of prints.

Too bad, but with more self-threading and rewinding projectors, the union didn't need Tyler anymore. Mister chapter president had to call Tyler in for a little sit-down.

The work was boring and the pay was crap, so the president of the united union of united projection operators independent and united theaters united said it was doing Tyler Durden a chapter favor by giving Tyler the diplomatic shaft.

Don't think of this as rejection. Think of it as downsizing.

Right up the butt mister chapter president himself says, "We appreciate your contribution to our success."

Oh, that wasn't a problem, Tyler said, and grinned. As long as the union kept sending a paycheck, he'd keep his mouth shut.

Tyler said, "Think of this as early retirement, with pension."

Tyler had handled hundreds of prints.

Movies had gone back to the distributor. Movies had gone back out in re-release. Comedy. Drama. Musicals. Romance. Action adventure.

Spliced with Tyler's single-frame flashes of pornography.

Sodomy. Fellatio. Cunnilingus. Bondage.

Tyler had nothing to lose.

Tyler was the pawn of the world, everybody's trash.

This is what Tyler rehearsed me to tell the manager of the Pressman Hotel, too.

At Tyler's other job, at the Pressman Hotel, Tyler said he was nobody. Nobody cared if he lived or died, and the feeling was fucking mutual. This is what Tyler told me to say in the hotel manager's office with security guards sitting outside the door.

Tyler and I stayed up late and traded stories after everything was over.

Right after he'd gone to the projectionist union, Tyler had me go and confront the manager of the Pressman Hotel.

Tyler and I were looking more and more like identical twins. Both of us had punched-out cheekbones, and our skin had lost its memory, and forgot where to slide back to after we were hit.

My bruises were from fight club, and Tyler's face was punched out of shape by the president of the projectionist union. After Tyler crawled out of the union offices, I went to see the manager of the Pressman Hotel.

I sat there, in the office of the manager of the Pressman Hotel.

I am Joe's Smirking Revenge.

The first thing the hotel manager said was I had three minutes. In the first thirty seconds, I told how I'd been peeing into soup, farting on crème brûlées, sneezing on braised endive, and now I wanted the hotel to send me a check every week equivalent to my average week's pay plus tips. In return, I wouldn't come to work anymore, and I wouldn't go to the newspapers or the public health people with a confused, tearful confession.

The headlines:

Troubled Waiter Admits Tainting Food.

Sure, I said, I might go to prison. They could hang me and yank my nuts off and drag me through the streets and flay my skin and burn me with lye, but the Pressman Hotel would always be known as the hotel where the richest people in the world ate pee.

Tyler's words coming out of my mouth.

And I used to be such a nice person.

At the projectionist union office, Tyler had laughed after the union president punched him. The one punch knocked Tyler out of his chair, and Tyler sat against the wall, laughing.

"Go ahead, you can't kill me," Tyler was laughing. "You stupid fuck. Beat the crap out of me, but you can't kill me."

You have too much to lose.

I have nothing.

You have everything.

Go ahead, right in the gut. Take another shot at my face. Cave in my teeth, but keep those paychecks coming. Crack my ribs, but if you miss one week's pay, I go public, and you and your little union go down under lawsuits from every theater owner and film distributor and mommy whose kid maybe saw a hard-on in *Bambi*.

"I am trash," Tyler said. "I am trash and shit and crazy to you and this whole fucking world," Tyler said to the union president. "You don't care where I live or how I feel, or what I eat or how I feed my kids or how I pay the doctor if I get sick, and yes I am stupid and bored and weak, but I am still your responsibility."

Sitting in the office at the Pressman Hotel, my fight club lips were still split into about ten segments. The butthole in my cheek looking at the manager of the Pressman Hotel, it was all pretty convincing.

Basically, I said the same stuff Tyler said.

After the union president had slugged Tyler to the floor, after mister president saw Tyler wasn't fighting back, his honor with his big Cadillac body bigger and stronger than he would ever really need, his honor hauled his wingtip back and kicked Tyler in the ribs and Tyler laughed. His honor shot the wingtip into Tyler's kidneys after Tyler curled into a ball, but Tyler was still laughing.

"Get it out," Tyler said. "Trust me. You'll feel a lot better. You'll feel great."

In the office of the Pressman Hotel, I asked the hotel manager if I could use his phone, and I dialed the number for the city desk at the newspaper. With the hotel manager watching, I said:

Hello, I said, I've committed a terrible crime against humanity as part of a political protest. My protest is over the exploitation of workers in the service industry.

If I went to prison, I wouldn't be just an unbalanced peon diddling in the soup. This would have heroic scale.

Robin Hood Waiter Champions Have-Nots.

This would be about a lot more than one hotel and one waiter.

The manager of the Pressman Hotel very gently took the receiver out of my hand. The manager said he didn't want me working here anymore, not the way I looked now.

I'm standing at the head of the manager's desk when I say, what?

You don't like the idea of *this?*

And without flinching, still looking at the manager, I roundhouse the fist at the centrifugal force end of my arm and slam fresh blood out of the cracked scabs in my nose.

For no reason at all, I remember the night Tyler and I had our first fight. *I want you to hit me as hard as you can.*

This isn't such a hard punch. I punch myself, again. It just looks good, all the blood, but I throw myself back against the wall to make a terrible noise and break the painting that hangs there.

The broken glass and frame and the painting of flowers and blood go to the floor with me clowning around. I'm being such a doofus. Blood gets on the carpet and I reach up and grip monster handprints of blood on the edge of the hotel manager's desk and say, please, help me, but I start to giggle.

Help me, please.

Please don't hit me, again.

I slip back to the floor and crawl my blood across the carpet. The first word I'm going to say is *please.* So I keep my lips shut. The monster drags itself across the lovely bouquets and garlands of the Oriental carpet. The blood falls out of my nose and slides down the back of my throat and into my mouth, hot. The monster crawls across the carpet, hot and picking up the lint and dust sticking to the blood on its claws. And it crawls close enough to grab the manager of the Pressman Hotel around his pinstriped ankle and say it.

Please.

Say it.

Please comes out in a bubble of blood.

Say it.

Please.

And the bubble pops blood all over.

And this is how Tyler was free to start a fight club every night of the week. After this there were seven fight clubs, and after that there were fifteen fight clubs, and after that, there were twenty-three fight clubs, and Tyler wanted more. There was always money coming in.

Please, I ask the manager of the Pressman Hotel, give me the money. And I giggle, again.

Please.

And please don't hit me, again.

You have so much, and I have nothing. And I start to climb my blood up the pinstriped legs of the manager of the Pressman Hotel who is leaning back, hard, with his hands on the windowsill behind him and even his thin lips retreating from his teeth.

The monster hooks its bloody claw in the waistband of the manager's pants, and pulls itself up to clutch the white starched shirt, and I wrap my bloody hands around the manager's smooth wrists.

Please. I smile big enough to split my lips.

There's a struggle as the manager screams and tries to get his hands away from me and my blood and my crushed nose, the filth sticking to the blood on both of us, and right then at our most excellent moment, the security guards decide to walk in.

16

IT'S IN THE newspaper today how somebody broke into offices between the tenth and fifteenth floors of the Hein Tower, and climbed out the office windows, and painted the south side of the building with a grinning five-story mask, and set fires so the window at the center of each huge eye blazed huge and alive and inescapable over the city at dawn.

In the picture on the front page of the newspaper, the face is an angry pumpkin, Japanese demon, dragon of avarice hanging in the sky, and the smoke is a witch's eyebrows or devil's horns. And people cried with their heads thrown back.

What did it mean?

And who would do this? And even after the fires were out, the face was still there, and it was worse. The empty eyes seemed to watch everyone in the street but at the same time were dead.

This stuff is in the newspaper more and more.

Of course you read this, and you want to know right away if it was part of Project Mayhem.

The newspaper says the police have no real leads. Youth gangs or space aliens, whoever it was could've died while crawling down ledges and dangling from windowsills with cans of black spray paint.

Was it the Mischief Committee or the Arson Committee? The giant face was probably their homework assignment from last week.

Tyler would know, but the first rule about Project Mayhem is you don't ask questions about Project Mayhem.

In the Assault Committee of Project Mayhem, this week Tyler says he ran everyone through what it would take to shoot a gun. All a gun does is focus an explosion in one direction.

At the last meeting of the Assault Committee, Tyler brought a gun and the yellow pages of the phone book. They meet in the basement where fight club meets on Saturday night. Each committee meets on a different night:

Arson meets on Monday.

Assault on Tuesday.

Mischief meets on Wednesday.

And Misinformation meets on Thursday.

Organized Chaos. The Bureaucracy of Anarchy. You figure it out. Support groups. Sort of.

So Tuesday night, the Assault Committee proposed events for the upcoming week, and Tyler read the proposals and gave the committee its homework.

By this time next week, each guy on the Assault Committee has to pick a fight where he won't come out a hero. And not in fight club. This is harder than it sounds. A man on the street will do anything not to fight.

The idea is to take some Joe on the street who's never been in a fight and recruit him. Let him experience winning for the first time in his life. Get him to explode. Give him permission to beat the crap out of you.

You can take it. If you win, you screwed up.

"What we have to do, people," Tyler told the committee, "is remind these guys what kind of power they still have."

This is Tyler's little pep talk. Then he opened each of the folded squares of paper in the cardboard box in front of him. This is how each committee proposes events for the upcoming week. Write the event on the committee tablet. Tear off the sheet, fold it, and put it in the box. Tyler checks out the proposals and throws out any bad ideas.

For each idea he throws out, Tyler puts a folded blank into the box.

Then everyone in the committee takes a paper out of the box. The way Tyler explained the process to me, if somebody draws a blank, he only has his homework to do that week.

If you draw a proposal, then you have to go to the import beer festival this weekend and push over a guy in a chemical toilet. You'll get extra favor if you get beat up for doing this. Or you have to attend the fashion show at the shopping center atrium and throw strawberry gelatin from the mezzanine.

If you get arrested, you're off the Assault Committee. If you laugh, you're off the committee.

Nobody knows who draws a proposal, and nobody except Tyler knows what all the proposals are and which are accepted and which proposals he throws in the trash. Later that week, you might read in the newspaper about an unidentified man, downtown, jumping the driver of a Jaguar convertible and steering the car into a fountain.

You have to wonder. Was this a committee proposal you could've drawn?

The next Tuesday night, you'll be looking around the Assault Committee meeting under the one light in the black fight club basement, and you're still wondering who forced the Jag into the fountain.

Who went to the roof of the art museum and snipered paint balls into the sculpture court reception?

Who painted the blazing demon mask on the Hein Tower?

The night of the Hein Tower assignment, you can picture a team of law clerks and bookkeepers or messengers sneaking into offices where they sat, every day. Maybe they were a little drunk even if it's against the rules in Project Mayhem, and they used passkeys where they could and used spray canisters of Freon to shatter lock cylinders so they could dangle, rappelling against the tower's brick facade, dropping, trusting each other to hold ropes, swinging, risking quick death in offices where every day they felt their lives end one hour at a time.

The next morning, these same clerks and assistant account reps would be in the crowd with their neatly combed heads thrown back, rummy without sleep but sober and wearing ties and listening to the crowd around them wonder, who would do this, and the police shout for everyone to please get back, now, as water ran down from the broken smoky center of each huge eye.

Tyler told me in secret that there's never more than four good proposals at a meeting so your chances of drawing a real proposal and not just a blank are about four in ten. There are twenty-five guys on the Assault Committee including Tyler. Everybody gets their homework: lose a fight in public; and each member draws for a proposal.

This week, Tyler told them, "Go out and buy a gun."

Tyler gave one guy the telephone-book yellow pages and told him to tear out an advertisement. Then pass the book to the next guy. No two guys should go to the same place to buy or shoot.

"This," Tyler said, and he took a gun out of his coat pocket, "this is a gun, and in two weeks, you should each of you have a gun about this size to bring to meeting.

"Better you should pay for it with cash," Tyler said. "Next meeting, you'll all trade guns and report the gun you bought as stolen."

Nobody asked anything. You don't ask questions is the first rule in Project Mayhem.

Tyler handed the gun around. It was so heavy for something so small, as if a giant thing like a mountain or a sun were collapsed and melted down to make this. The committee guys held it by two fingers. Everyone wanted to ask if it was loaded, but the second rule of Project Mayhem is you don't ask questions.

Maybe it was loaded, maybe not. Maybe we should always assume the worst.

"A gun," Tyler said, "is simple and perfect. You just draw the trigger back."

The third rule in Project Mayhem is no excuses.

"The trigger," Tyler said, "frees the hammer, and the hammer strikes the powder."

The fourth rule is no lies.

"The explosion blasts a metal slug off the open end of the shell, and the barrel of the gun focuses the exploding powder and the rocketing slug," Tyler said, "like a man out of a cannon, like a missile out of a silo, like your jism, in one direction."

When Tyler invented Project Mayhem, Tyler said the goal of Project Mayhem had nothing to do with other people. Tyler didn't care if other people got hurt or not. The goal was to teach each man in the project that he had the power to control history. We, each of us, can take control of the world.

It was at fight club that Tyler invented Project Mayhem.

I tagged a first-timer one night at fight club. That Saturday night, a young guy with an angel's face came to his first fight club, and I tagged him for a fight. That's the rule. If it's your first night in fight club, you have to fight. I knew that so I tagged him because the insomnia was on again, and I was in a mood to destroy something beautiful.

Since most of my face never gets a chance to heal, I've got nothing to lose in the looks department. My boss, at work, he asked me what I was doing about the hole through my cheek that never heals. When I drink coffee, I told him, I put two fingers over the hole so it won't leak.

There's a sleeper hold that gives somebody just enough air to stay awake, and that night at fight club I hit our first-timer and hammered that beautiful mister angel face, first with the bony knuckles of my fist like a pounding molar, and then the knotted tight butt of my fist after my knuckles were raw from his teeth stuck through his lips. Then the kid fell through my arms in a heap.

Tyler told me later that he'd never seen me destroy something so completely. That night, Tyler knew he had to take fight club up a notch or shut it down.

Tyler said, sitting at breakfast the next morning, "You looked like a maniac, Psycho-Boy. Where did you go?"

I said I felt like crap and not relaxed at all. I didn't get any kind of a buzz. Maybe I'd developed a jones. You can build up a tolerance to fighting, and maybe I needed to move on to something bigger.

It was that morning, Tyler invented Project Mayhem.

Tyler asked what I was really fighting.

What Tyler says about being the crap and the slaves of history, that's how I felt. I wanted to destroy everything beautiful I'd never have. Burn the Amazon rain forests. Pump chlorofluorocarbons straight up to gobble the ozone. Open the dump valves on supertankers and uncap offshore oil wells. I wanted to kill all the fish I couldn't afford to eat, and smother the French beaches I'd never see.

I wanted the whole world to hit bottom.

Pounding that kid, I really wanted to put a bullet between the eyes of every endangered panda that wouldn't screw to save its species and every whale or dolphin that gave up and ran itself aground.

Don't think of this as extinction. Think of this as downsizing.

For thousands of years, human beings had screwed up and trashed and crapped on this planet, and now history expected me to clean up after everyone. I have to wash out and flatten my soup cans. And account for every drop of used motor oil.

And I have to foot the bill for nuclear waste and buried gasoline tanks and landfilled toxic sludge dumped a generation before I was born.

I held the face of mister angel like a baby or a football in the crook of my arm and bashed him with my knuckles, bashed him until his teeth broke through his lips. Bashed him with my elbow after that until he fell through my arms into a heap at my feet. Until the skin was pounded thin across his cheekbones and turned black.

I wanted to breathe smoke.

Birds and deer are a silly luxury, and all the fish should be floating.

I wanted to burn the Louvre. I'd do the Elgin Marbles with a sledge-hammer and wipe my ass with the *Mona Lisa*. This is my world, now.

This is my world, my world, and those ancient people are dead.

It was at breakfast that morning that Tyler invented Project Mayhem.

We wanted to blast the world free of history.

We were eating breakfast in the house on Paper Street, and Tyler said, picture yourself planting radishes and seed potatoes on the fifteenth green of a forgotten golf course.

You'll hunt elk through the damp canyon forests around the ruins of Rockefeller Center, and dig clams next to the skeleton of the Space Needle leaning at a forty-five-degree angle. We'll paint the skyscrapers with huge totem faces and goblin tikis, and every evening what's left of mankind will retreat to empty zoos and lock itself in cages as protection against bears and big cats and wolves that pace and watch us from outside the cage bars at night.

"Recycling and speed limits are bullshit," Tyler said. "They're like someone who quits smoking on his deathbed."

It's Project Mayhem that's going to save the world. A cultural ice age. A prematurely induced dark age. Project Mayhem will force humanity to go dormant or into remission long enough for the Earth to recover.

"You justify anarchy," Tyler says. "You figure it out."

Like fight club does with clerks and box boys, Project Mayhem will break up civilization so we can make something better out of the world.

"Imagine," Tyler said, "stalking elk past department store windows and stinking racks of beautiful rotting dresses and tuxedos on hangers; you'll wear leather clothes that will last you the rest of your life, and you'll climb the wrist-thick kudzu vines that wrap the Sears Tower. Jack and the beanstalk, you'll climb up through the dripping forest canopy and the air will be so clean you'll see tiny figures pounding corn and laying strips of venison to dry in the empty car pool lane of an abandoned superhighway stretching eight-lanes-wide and August-hot for a thousand miles."

This was the goal of Project Mayhem, Tyler said, the complete and right-away destruction of civilization.

What comes next in Project Mayhem, nobody except Tyler knows. The second rule is you don't ask questions.

"Don't get any bullets," Tyler told the Assault Committee. "And just so you don't worry about it, yes, you're going to have to kill someone."

Arson. Assault. Mischief and Misinformation.

No questions. No questions. No excuses and no lies.

The fifth rule about Project Mayhem is you have to trust Tyler.

17

M Y B O S S B R I N G S another sheet of paper to my desk and sets it at my elbow. I don't even wear a tie anymore. My boss is wearing his blue tie, so it must be a Thursday. The door to my boss's office is always closed now, and we haven't traded more than two words any day since he found the fight club rules in the copy machine and I maybe implied I might gut him with a shotgun blast. Just me clowning around, again.

Or, I might call the Compliance people at the Department of Transportation. There's a front seat mounting bracket that never passed collision testing before it went into production.

If you know where to look, there are bodies buried everywhere.

Morning, I say.

He says, "Morning."

Set at my elbow is another for-my-eyes-only important secret document Tyler wanted me to type up and copy. A week ago, Tyler was pacing out the dimensions of the basement of the rented house on Paper Street. It's sixty-five shoe lengths front to back and forty shoe lengths side to side. Tyler was thinking out loud. Tyler asked me, "What is six times seven?"

Forty-two.

"And forty-two times three?"

One hundred and twenty-six.

Tyler gave me a handwritten list of notes and said to type it and make seventy-two copies.

Why that many?

"Because," Tyler said, "that's how many guys can sleep in the basement, if we put them in triple-decker army surplus bunk beds."

I asked, what about their stuff?

Tyler said, "They won't bring anything more than what's on the list, and it should all fit under a mattress."

The list my boss finds in the copy machine, the copy machine counter still set for seventy-two copies, the list says:

"Bringing the required items does not guarantee admission to training, but no applicant will be considered unless he arrives equipped with the following items and exactly five hundred dollars cash for personal burial money."

It costs at least three hundred dollars to cremate an indigent corpse, Tyler told me, and the price was going up. Anyone who dies without at least this much money, their body goes to an autopsy class.

This money must always be carried in the student's shoe so if the student is ever killed, his death will not be a burden on Project Mayhem.

In addition, the applicant has to arrive with the following:

Two black shirts.

Two black pair of trousers.

One pair of heavy black shoes.

Two pair of black socks and two pair of plain underwear.

One heavy black coat.

This includes the clothes the applicant has on his back.

One white towel.

One army surplus cot mattress.

One white plastic mixing bowl.

At my desk, with my boss still standing there, I pick up the original list and tell him, thanks. My boss goes into his office, and I set to work playing solitaire on my computer.

After work, I give Tyler the copies, and days go by. I go to work.

I come home.

I go to work.

I come home, and there's a guy standing on our front porch. The guy's at the front door with his second black shirt and pants in a brown paper sack and he's got the last three items, a white towel, an army surplus mattress, and a plastic bowl, set on the porch railing. From an upstairs window, Tyler and I peek out at the guy, and Tyler tells me to send the guy away.

"He's too young," Tyler says.

The guy on the porch is mister angel face whom I tried to destroy the night Tyler invented Project Mayhem. Even with his two black eyes and blond crew cut, you see his tough pretty scowl without wrinkles or scars. Put him in a dress and make him smile, and he'd be a woman. Mister angel just stands his toes against the front door, just looks straight ahead into the splintering wood with his hands at his sides, wearing black shoes, black shirt, black pair of trousers.

"Get rid of him," Tyler tells me. "He's too young."

I ask how young is too young?

"It doesn't matter," Tyler says. "If the applicant is young, we tell him he's too young. If he's fat, he's too fat. If he's old, he's too old.

Thin, he's too thin. White, he's too white. Black, he's too black."

This is how Buddhist temples have tested applicants going back for bah-zillion years, Tyler says. You tell the applicant to go away, and if his resolve is so strong that he waits at the entrance without food or shelter or encouragement for three days, then and only then can he enter and begin the training.

So I tell mister angel he's too young, but at lunchtime he's still there. After lunch, I go out and beat mister angel with a broom and kick the guy's sack out into the street. From upstairs, Tyler watches me stick-ball the broom upside the kid's ear, the kid just standing there, then I kick his stuff into the gutter and scream.

Go away, I'm screaming. Haven't you heard? You're too young. You'll never make it, I scream. Come back in a couple years and apply again. Just go. Just get off my porch.

The next day, the guy is still there, and Tyler goes out to go, "I'm sorry." Tyler says he's sorry he told the guy about training, but the guy is really too young, and would he please just go.

Good cop. Bad cop.

I scream at the poor guy, again. Then, six hours later, Tyler goes out and says he's sorry, but no. The guy has to leave. Tyler says he's going to call the police if the guy won't leave.

And the guy stays.

And his clothes are still in the gutter. The wind takes the torn paper sack away.

And the guy stays.

On the third day, another applicant is at the front door. Mister angel is still there, and Tyler goes down and just tells mister angel, "Come in. Get your stuff out of the street and come in."

To the new guy, Tyler says, he's sorry but there's been a mistake. The new guy is too old to train here, and would he please leave.

I go to work every day. I come home, and every day there's one or two guys waiting on the front porch. These new guys don't make eye contact. I shut the door and leave them on the porch. This happens every day for a while, and sometimes the applicants will leave, but most times, the applicants stick it out until the third day, until most of the seventy-two bunk beds Tyler and I bought and set up in the basement are full.

One day, Tyler gives me five hundred dollars in cash and tells me to keep it in my shoe all the time. My personal burial money. This is another old Buddhist monastery thing.

I come home from work now, and the house is filled with strangers that Tyler has accepted. All of them working. The whole first floor turns into a kitchen and a soap factory. The bathroom is never empty. Teams of men disappear for a few days and come home with red rubber bags of thin, watery fat.

One night, Tyler comes upstairs to find me hiding in my room and says, "Don't bother them. They all know what to do. It's part of Project Mayhem. No one guy understands the whole plan, but each guy is trained to do one simple task perfectly."

The rule in Project Mayhem is you have to trust Tyler.

Then Tyler's gone.

Teams of Project Mayhem guys render fat all day. I'm not sleeping. All night I hear other teams mix the lye and cut the bars and bake the bars of soap on cookie sheets, then wrap each bar in tissue and seal it with the Paper Street Soap Company label. Everyone except me seems to know what to do, and Tyler is never home.

I hug the walls, being a mouse trapped in this clockwork of silent men with the energy of trained monkeys, cooking and working and sleeping in teams. Pull a lever. Push a button. A team of space monkeys cooks meals all day, and all day, teams of space monkeys are eating out of the plastic bowls they brought with them.

One morning I'm leaving for work and Big Bob's on the front

porch wearing black shoes and a black shirt and pants. I ask, has he seen Tyler lately? Did Tyler send him here?

"The first rule about Project Mayhem," Big Bob says with his heels together and his back ramrod straight, "is you don't ask questions about Project Mayhem."

So what brainless little honor has Tyler assigned him, I ask. There are guys whose job is to just boil rice all day or wash out eating bowls or clean the crapper. All day. Has Tyler promised Big Bob enlightenment if he spends sixteen hours a day wrapping bars of soap?

Big Bob doesn't say anything.

I go to work. I come home, and Big Bob's still on the porch. I don't sleep all night, and the next morning, Big Bob's out tending the garden.

Before I leave for work, I ask Big Bob, who let him in? Who assigned him this task? Did he see Tyler? Was Tyler here last night?

Big Bob says, "The first rule in Project Mayhem is you don't talk—"

I cut him off. I say, yeah. Yeah, yeah, yeah, yeah, yeah.

And while I'm at work, teams of space monkeys dig up the muddy lawn around the house and cut the dirt with Epsom salts to lower the acidity, and spade in loads of free steer manure from the stockyards and bags of hair clippings from barber shops to ward off moles and mice and boost the protein in the soil.

At any time of the night, space monkeys from some slaughterhouse come home with bags of blood meal to boost the iron in the soil and bone meal to boost the phosphorus.

Teams of space monkeys plant basil and thyme and lettuce and starts of witch hazel and eucalyptus and mock orange and mint in a kaleidoscope knot pattern. A rose window in every shade of green. And other teams go out at night and kill the slugs and snails by candlelight. Another team of space monkeys picks only the most perfect leaves and juniper berries to boil for a natural dye. Comfrey because it's a natural disinfectant. Violet leaves because they cure headaches and sweet woodruff because it gives soap a cut-grass smell.

In the kitchen are bottles of 80-proof vodka to make the translucent rose geranium and brown sugar soap and the patchouli soap, and I steal a bottle of vodka and spend my personal burial money on cigarettes. Marla shows up. We talk about the plants. Marla and I walk on raked gravel paths through the kaleidoscope green patterns of the garden, drinking and smoking. We talk about her breasts. We talk about everything except Tyler Durden.

And one day it's in the newspaper how a team of men wearing black had stormed through a better neighborhood and a luxury car dealership slamming baseball bats against the front bumpers of cars so the air bags inside would explode in a powdery mess with their car alarms screaming.

At the Paper Street Soap Company, other teams pick the petals from roses or anemones and lavender and pack the flowers into boxes with a cake of pure tallow that will absorb their scent for making soap with a flower smell.

Marla tells me about the plants.

The rose, Marla tells me, is a natural astringent.

Some of the plants have obituary names: Iris, Basil, Rue, Rosemary, and Verbena. Some, like meadowsweet and cowslips, sweet flag and spikenard, are like the names of Shakespeare fairies. Deer tongue with its sweet vanilla smell. Witch hazel, another natural astringent.

Orrisroot, the wild Spanish iris.

Every night, Marla and I walk in the garden until I'm sure that Tyler's not coming home that night. Right behind us is always a space monkey trailing us to pick up the twist of balm or rue or mint Marla crushes under my nose. A dropped cigarette butt. The space monkey rakes the path behind him to erase our ever being there.

And one night in an uptown square park, another group of men poured gasoline around every tree and from tree to tree and set a perfect little forest fire. It was in the newspaper, how townhouse windows across the street from the fire melted, and parked cars farted and settled on melted flat tires.

Tyler's rented house on Paper Street is a living thing wet on the inside from so many people sweating and breathing. So many people are moving inside, the house moves.

Another night that Tyler didn't come home, someone was drilling bank machines and pay telephones and then screwing lube fittings into the drilled holes and using a grease gun to pump the bank machines and pay telephones full of axle grease or vanilla pudding.

And Tyler was never at home, but after a month a few of the space monkeys had Tyler's kiss burned into the back of their hand. Then those space monkeys were gone, too, and new ones were on the front porch to replace them.

And every day, the teams of men came and went in different cars. You never saw the same car twice. One evening, I hear Marla on the front porch, telling a space monkey, "I'm here to see Tyler. Tyler Durden. He lives here. I'm his friend."

The space monkey says, "I'm sorry, but you're too . . . ," and he pauses, "you're too young to train here."

Marla says, "Get screwed."

"Besides," the space monkey says, "you haven't brought the required items: two black shirts, two pair of black pants—"

Marla screams, "Tyler!"

"One pair of heavy black shoes."

"Tyler!"

"Two pair of black socks and two pair of plain underwear."

"Tyler!"

And I hear the front door slam shut. Marla doesn't wait the three days.

Most days, after work, I come home and make a peanut butter sandwich.

When I come home, one space monkey is reading to the assembled space monkeys who sit covering the whole first floor. "You are not a beautiful and unique snowflake. You are the same decaying organic matter as everyone else, and we are all part of the same compost pile."

The space monkey continues, "Our culture has made us all the same. No one is truly white or black or rich, anymore. We all want the same. Individually, we are nothing."

The reader stops when I walk in to make my sandwich, and all the space monkeys sit silent as if I were alone. I say, don't bother. I've already read it. I typed it.

Even my boss has probably read it.

We're all just a big bunch of crap, I say. Go ahead. Play your little game. Don't mind me.

The space monkeys wait in quiet while I make my sandwich and take another bottle of vodka and go up the stairs. Behind me I hear, "You are not a beautiful and unique snowflake."

I am Joe's Broken Heart because Tyler's dumped me. Because my father dumped me. Oh, I could go on and on.

Some nights, after work, I go to a different fight club in the basement of a bar or garage, and I ask if anybody's seen Tyler Durden.

In every new fight club, someone I've never met is standing under the one light in the center of the darkness, surrounded by men, and reading Tyler's words.

The first rule about fight club is you don't talk about fight club.

When the fights get started, I take the club leader aside and ask if he's seen Tyler. I live with Tyler, I say, and he hasn't been home for a while.

The guy's eyes get big and he asks, do I really know Tyler Durden?

This happens in most of the new fight clubs. Yes, I say, I'm best buddies with Tyler. Then, everybody all of a sudden wants to shake my hand.

These new guys stare at the butthole in my cheek and the black skin on my face, yellow and green around the edges, and they call me sir. No, sir. Not hardly, sir. Nobody they know's ever met Tyler Durden. Friends of friends met Tyler Durden, and they founded this chapter of fight club, sir.

Then they wink at me.

Nobody they know has ever seen Tyler Durden.

Sir.

Is it true, everybody asks. Is Tyler Durden building an army? That's the word. Does Tyler Durden only sleep one hour a night? Rumor has it that Tyler's on the road starting fight clubs all over the country. What's next, everybody wants to know.

The meetings for Project Mayhem have moved to bigger basements because each committee—Arson, Assault, Mischief, and Misinformation—gets bigger as more guys graduate out of fight club. Each committee has a leader, and even the leaders don't know where Tyler's at. Tyler calls them every week on the phone.

Everybody on Project Mayhem wants to know what's next.

Where are we going?

What is there to look forward to?

On Paper Street, Marla and I walk through the garden at night with our bare feet, every step brushing up the smell of sage and lemon verbena and rose geranium. Black shirts and black pants hunch around us with candles, lifting plant leaves to kill a snail or slug. Marla asks, what's going on here?

Tufts of hair surface beside the dirt clods. Hair and shit. Bone meal and blood meal. The plants are growing faster than the space monkeys can cut them back.

Marla asks, "What are you going to do?"

What's the word?

In the dirt is a shining spot of gold, and I kneel down to see. What's going to happen next, I don't know, I tell Marla.

It looks like we've both been dumped.

In the corner of my eye, the space monkeys pace around in black, each one hunched over his candle. The little spot of gold in the dirt is a molar with a gold filling. Next to it surface two more molars with silver amalgam fillings. It's a jawbone.

I say, no, I can't say what's going to happen. And I push the one, two, three molars into the dirt and hair and shit and bone and blood where Marla won't see.

18

THIS FRIDAY NIGHT, I fall asleep at my desk at work.

When I wake up with my face and my crossed arms on my desktop, the telephone is ringing, and everyone else is gone. A telephone was ringing in my dream, and it's not clear if reality slipped into my dream or if my dream is slopping over into reality.

I answer the phone, Compliance and Liability.

That's my department. Compliance and Liability.

The sun is going down, and piled-up storm clouds the size of Wyoming and Japan are headed our way. It's not like I have a window at work. All the outside walls are floor-to-ceiling glass. Everything where I work is floor-to-ceiling glass. Everything is vertical blinds. Everything is industrial low-pile gray carpet spotted with little tombstone monuments where the PCs plug into the network. Everything is a maze of cubicles boxed in with fences of upholstered plywood.

A vacuum cleaner hums somewhere.

My boss is gone on vacation. He sent me an E-mail and then disappeared. I'm to prepare for a formal review in two weeks. Reserve a conference room. Get all my ducks in a row. Update my résumé. That sort of thing. They're building a case against me.

I am Joe's Complete Lack of Surprise.

I've been behaving miserably.

I pick up the phone, and it's Tyler, and he says, "Go outside, there's some guys waiting for you in the parking lot."

I ask, who are they?

"They're all waiting," Tyler says.

I smell gasoline on my hands.

Tyler goes, "Hit the road. They have a car, outside. They have a Cadillac."

I'm still asleep.

Here, I'm not sure if Tyler is my dream.

Or if I am Tyler's dream.

I sniff the gasoline on my hands. There's nobody else around, and I get up and walk out to the parking lot.

A guy in fight club works on cars so he's parked at the curb in somebody's black Corniche, and all I can do is look at it, all black and gold, this huge cigarette case ready to drive me somewhere. This mechanic guy who gets out of the car tells me not to worry, he switched the plates with another car in the long-term parking lot at the airport.

Our fight club mechanic says he can start anything. Two wires twist out of the steering column. Touch the wires to each other, you complete the circuit to the starter solenoid, you got a car to joyride.

Either that, or you could hack the key code through a dealership.

Three space monkeys are sitting in the back seat wearing their black shirts and black pants. See no evil. Hear no evil. Speak no evil.

I ask, so where's Tyler?

The fight club mechanic guy is holding the Cadillac open chauffeur style for me. The mechanic is tall and all bones with shoulders that remind you of a telephone pole crossbar.

I ask, are we going to see Tyler?

Waiting for me in the middle of the front seat is a birthday cake with candles ready to be lit. I get in. We start driving.

Even a week after fight club, you've got no problem driving inside the speed limit. Maybe you've been passing black shit, internal injuries, for two days, but you are so cool. Other cars drive around you. Cars tailgate. You get the finger from other drivers. Total strangers hate you. It's absolutely nothing personal. After fight club, you're so relaxed, you just cannot care. You don't even turn the radio on. Maybe your ribs stab along a hairline fracture every time you take a breath. Cars behind you blink their lights. The sun is going down, orange and gold.

The mechanic is there, driving. The birthday cake is on the seat between us.

It's one scary fuck to see guys like our mechanic at fight club. Skinny guys, they never go limp. They fight until they're burger. White guys like skeletons dipped in yellow wax with tattoos, black men like dried meat, these guys usually hang together, the way you can picture them at Narcotics Anonymous. They never say, stop. It's like they're all energy, shaking so fast they blur around the edges, these guys in recovery from something. As if the only choice they have left is how they're going to die and they want to die in a fight.

They have to fight each other, these guys.

Nobody else will tag them for a fight, and they can't tag anybody except another twitching skinny, all bones and rush, since nobody else will register to fight them.

Guys watching don't even yell when guys like our mechanic go at each other.

All you hear is the fighters breathing through their teeth, hands slapping for a hold, the whistle and impact when fists hammer and hammer on thin hollow ribs, point-blank in a clinch. You see tendons and muscle and veins under the skin of these guys jump. Their skin shines, sweating, corded, and wet under the one light.

Ten, fifteen minutes disappear. Their smell, they sweat and these guys' smell, it reminds you of fried chicken.

Twenty minutes of fight club will go by. Finally, one guy will go down.

After a fight, two drug recovery guys will hang together for the rest of the night, wasted and smiling from fighting so hard.

Since fight club, this mechanic guy is always hanging around the house on Paper Street. Wants me to hear the song he wrote. Wants me to see the birdhouse he built. The guy showed me a picture of some girl and asked me if she was pretty enough to marry.

Sitting in the front seat of the Corniche, the guy says, "Did you see this cake I made for you? I made this."

It's not my birthday.

"Some oil was getting by the rings," the mechanic guy says, "but I changed the oil and the air filter. I checked the valve lash and the timing. It's supposed to rain, tonight, so I changed the blades."

I ask, what's Tyler been planning?

The mechanic opens the ashtray and pushes the cigarette lighter in. He says, "Is this a test? Are you testing us?"

Where's Tyler?

"The first rule about fight club is you don't talk about fight club," the mechanic says. "And the last rule about Project Mayhem is you don't ask questions."

So what can he tell me?

He says, "What you have to understand, is your father was your model for God."

Behind us, my job and my office are smaller, smaller, smaller, gone.

I sniff the gasoline on my hands.

The mechanic says, "If you're male and you're Christian and living in America, your father is your model for God. And if you never know your father, if your father bails out or dies or is never at home, what do you believe about God?"

This is all Tyler Durden dogma. Scrawled on bits of paper while I was asleep and given to me to type and photocopy at work. I've read it all. Even my boss has probably read it all.

"What you end up doing," the mechanic says, "is you spend your life searching for a father and God."

"What you have to consider," he says, "is the possibility that God doesn't like you. Could be, God hates us. This is not the worst thing that can happen."

How Tyler saw it was that getting God's attention for being bad was better than getting no attention at all. Maybe because God's hate is better than His indifference.

If you could be either God's worst enemy or nothing, which would you choose?

We are God's middle children, according to Tyler Durden, with no special place in history and no special attention.

Unless we get God's attention, we have no hope of damnation or redemption.

Which is worse, hell or nothing?

Only if we're caught and punished can we be saved.

"Burn the Louvre," the mechanic says, "and wipe your ass with the *Mona Lisa*. This way at least, God would know our names."

The lower you fall, the higher you'll fly. The farther you run, the more God wants you back.

"If the prodigal son had never left home," the mechanic says, "the fatted calf would still be alive."

It's not enough to be numbered with the grains of sand on the beach and the stars in the sky.

The mechanic merges the black Corniche onto the old bypass highway with no passing lane, and already a line of trucks strings together behind us, going the legal speed limit. The Corniche fills up with the headlights behind us, and there we are, talking, reflected in the inside of the windshield. Driving inside the speed limit. As fast as the law allows.

A law is a law, Tyler would say. Driving too fast was the same as setting a fire was the same as planting a bomb was the same as shooting a man.

A criminal is a criminal is a criminal.

"Last week, we could've filled another four fight clubs," the mechanic says. "Maybe Big Bob can take over running the next chapter if we find a bar."

So next week, he'll go through the rules with Big Bob and give him a fight club of his own.

From now on, when a leader starts fight club, when everyone is standing around the light in the center of the basement, waiting, the leader should walk around and around the outside edge of the crowd, in the dark.

I ask, who made up the new rules? Is it Tyler?

The mechanic smiles and says, "You know who makes up the rules."

The new rule is that nobody should be the center of fight club, he says. Nobody's the center of fight club except the two men fighting. The leader's voice will yell, walking slowly around the crowd, out in the darkness. The men in the crowd will stare at other men across the empty center of the room.

This is how it will be in all the fight clubs.

Finding a bar or a garage to host a new fight club isn't tough; the first bar, the one where the original fight club still meets, they make their month's rent in just one fight club Saturday night.

According to the mechanic, another new fight club rule is that fight club will always be free. It will never cost to get in. The mechanic yells out the driver's window into the oncoming traffic and the night wind pouring down the side of the car: "We want you, not your money."

The mechanic yells out the window, "As long as you're at fight club, you're not how much money you've got in the bank. You're not your job. You're not your family, and you're not who you tell yourself."

The mechanic yells into the wind, "You're not your name."

A space monkey in the back seat picks it up: "You're not your problems."

The mechanic yells, "You're not your problems."

A space monkey shouts, "You're not your age."

The mechanic yells, "You're not your age."

Here, the mechanic swerves us into the oncoming lane, filling the car with headlights through the windshield, cool as ducking jabs. One car and then another comes at us head-on screaming its horn and the mechanic swerves just enough to miss each one.

Headlights come at us, bigger and bigger, horns screaming, and the mechanic cranes forward into the glare and noise and screams, "You are not your hopes."

No one takes up the yell.

This time, the car coming head-on swerves in time to save us.

Another car comes on, headlights blinking high, low, high, low, horn blaring, and the mechanic screams, "You will not be saved."

The mechanic doesn't swerve, but the head-on car swerves.

Another car, and the mechanic screams, "We are all going to die, someday."

This time, the oncoming car swerves, but the mechanic swerves back into its path. The car swerves, and the mechanic matches it, head-on, again.

You melt and swell at that moment. For that moment, nothing matters. Look up at the stars and you're gone. Not your luggage. Nothing matters. Not your bad breath. The windows are dark outside and the horns are blaring around you. The headlights are flashing high and low and high in your face, and you will never have to go to work again.

You will never have to get another haircut.

"Quick," the mechanic says.

The car swerves again, and the mechanic swerves back into its path.

"What," he says, "what will you wish you'd done before you died?"

With the oncoming car screaming its horn and the mechanic so cool he even looks away to look at me beside him in the front seat, and he says, "Ten seconds to impact.

"Nine.

"In eight.

"Seven.

"In six."

My job, I say. I wish I'd quit my job.

The scream goes by as the car swerves and the mechanic doesn't swerve to hit it.

More lights are coming at us just ahead, and the mechanic turns to the three monkeys in the back seat. "Hey, space monkeys," he says, "you see how the game's played. Fess up now or we're all dead."

A car passes us on the right with a bumper sticker saying, "I Drive Better When I'm Drunk." The newspaper says thousands of these bumper stickers just appeared on cars one morning. Other bumper stickers said things like "Make Mine Veal."

"Drunk Drivers Against Mothers."

"Recycle All the Animals."

Reading the newspaper, I knew the Misinformation Committee had pulled this. Or the Mischief Committee.

Sitting beside me, our clean and sober fight club mechanic tells me, yeah, the Drunk bumper stickers are part of Project Mayhem.

The three space monkeys are quiet in the back seat.

The Mischief Committee is printing airline pocket cards that show passengers fighting each other for oxygen masks while their jetliner flames down toward the rocks at a thousand miles an hour.

Mischief and Misinformation Committees are racing each other to develop a computer virus that will make automated bank tellers sick enough to vomit storms of ten- and twenty-dollar bills.

The cigarette lighter in the dash pops out hot, and the mechanic tells me to light the candles on the birthday cake.

I light the candles, and the cake shimmers under a little halo of fire.

"What will you wish you'd done before you died?" the mechanic says and swerves us into the path of a truck coming head-on. The truck hits the air horn, bellowing one long blast after another as the truck's headlights, like a sunrise, come brighter and brighter to sparkle off the mechanic's smile.

"Make your wish, quick," he says to the rearview mirror where the three space monkeys are sitting in the back seat. "We've got five seconds to oblivion.

"One," he says.

"Two."

The truck is everything in front of us, blinding bright and roaring.

"Three."

"Ride a horse," comes from the back seat.

"Build a house," comes another voice.

"Get a tattoo."

The mechanic says, "Believe in me and you shall die, forever."

Too late, the truck swerves and the mechanic swerves but the rear of our Corniche fishtails against one end of the truck's front bumper.

Not that I know this at the time, what I know is the lights, the truck headlights blink out into darkness and I'm thrown first against the passenger door and then against the birthday cake and the mechanic behind the steering wheel.

The mechanic's lying crabbed on the wheel to keep it straight and the birthday candles snuff out. In one perfect second there's no light inside the warm black leather car and our shouts all hit the same deep note, the same low moan of the truck's air horn, and we have no control, no choice, no direction, and no escape and we're dead.

My wish right now is for me to die. I am nothing in the world compared to Tyler.

I am helpless.

I am stupid, and all I do is want and need things.

My tiny life. My little shit job. My Swedish furniture. I never, no, never told anyone this, but before I met Tyler, I was planning to buy a dog and name it "Entourage."

This is how bad your life can get.

Kill me.

I grab the steering wheel and crank us back into traffic.

Now.

Prepare to evacuate soul.

Now.

The mechanic wrestles the wheel toward the ditch, and I wrestle to fucking die.

Now. The amazing miracle of death, when one second you're walking and talking, and the next second, you're an object.

I am nothing, and not even that.

Cold.

Invisible.

I smell leather. My seat belt feels twisted like a straitjacket around me, and when I try to sit up, I hit my head against the steering wheel. This hurts more than it should. My head is resting in the mechanic's lap, and as I look up, my eyes adjust to see the mechanic's face high over me, smiling, driving, and I can see stars outside the driver's window.

My hands and face are sticky with something.

Blood?

Buttercream frosting.

The mechanic looks down. "Happy Birthday."

I smell smoke and remember the birthday cake.

"I almost broke the steering wheel with your head," he says.

Just nothing else, just the night air and the smell of smoke, and the stars and the mechanic smiling and driving, my head in his lap, all of a sudden I don't feel like I have to sit up.

Where's the cake?

The mechanic says, "On the floor."

Just the night air and the smell of smoke is heavier.

Did I get my wish?

Up above me, outlined against the stars in the window, the face smiles. "Those birthday candles," he says, "they're the kind that never go out."

In the starlight, my eyes adjust enough to see smoke braiding up from little fires all around us in the carpet.

19

THE FIGHT CLUB mechanic is standing on the gas, raging behind the wheel in his quiet way, and we still have something important to do, tonight.

One thing I'll have to learn before the end of civilization is how to look at the stars and tell where I'm going. Things are quiet as driving a Cadillac through outer space. We must be off the freeway. The three guys in the back seat are passed out or asleep.

"You had a near-life experience," the mechanic says.

He takes one hand off the steering wheel and touches the long welt where my forehead bounced off the steering wheel. My forehead is swelling enough to shut both my eyes, and he runs a cold fingertip down the length of the swelling. The Corniche hits a bump and the pain seems to bump out over my eyes like the shadow from the brim of a cap. Our twisted rear springs and bumper bark and creak in the quiet around our rush down the night road.

The mechanic says how the back bumper of the Corniche is hanging by its ligaments, how it was torn almost free when it caught an end of the truck's front bumper.

I ask, is tonight part of his homework for Project Mayhem?

"Part of it," he says. "I had to make four human sacrifices, and I have to pick up a load of fat."

Fat?

"For the soap."

What is Tyler planning?

The mechanic starts talking, and it's pure Tyler Durden.

"I see the strongest and the smartest men who have ever lived," he says, his face outlined against the stars in the driver's window, "and these men are pumping gas and waiting tables."

The drop of his forehead, his brow, the slope of his nose, his eyelashes and the curve of his eyes, the plastic profile of his mouth, talking, these are all outlined in black against the stars.

"If we could put these men in training camps and finish raising them.

"All a gun does is focus an explosion in one direction.

"You have a class of young strong men and women, and they want to give their lives to something. Advertising has these people chasing cars and clothes they don't need. Generations have been working in jobs they hate, just so they can buy what they don't really need.

"We don't have a great war in our generation, or a great depression, but we do, we have a great war of the spirit. We have a great revolution against the culture. The great depression is our lives. We have a spiritual depression.

"We have to show these men and women freedom by enslaving them, and show them courage by frightening them.

"Napoleon bragged that he could train men to sacrifice their lives for a scrap of ribbon.

"Imagine, when we call a strike and everyone refuses to work until we redistribute the wealth of the world.

"Imagine hunting elk through the damp canyon forests around the ruins of Rockefeller Center.

"What you said about your job," the mechanic says, "did you really mean it?"

Yeah, I meant it.

"That's why we're on the road, tonight," he says.

We're a hunting party, and we're hunting for fat.

We're going to the medical waste dump.

We're going to the medical waste incinerator, and there among the discarded surgical drapes and wound dressings, and ten-year-old tumors and intraveneous tubes and discarded needles, scary stuff, really scary stuff, among the blood samples and amputated tidbits, we'll find more money than we can haul away in one night, even if we were driving a dump truck.

We'll find enough money to load this Corniche down to the axle stops.

"Fat," the mechanic says, "liposuctioned fat sucked out of the richest thighs in America. The richest, fattest thighs in the world."

Our goal is the big red bags of liposuctioned fat we'll haul back to Paper Street and render and mix with lye and rosemary and sell back to the very people who paid to have it sucked out. At twenty bucks a bar, these are the only folks who can afford it.

"The richest, creamiest fat in the world, the fat of the land," he says. "That makes tonight a kind of Robin Hood thing."

The little wax fires sputter in the carpet.

"While we're there," he says, "we're supposed to look for some of those hepatitis bugs, too."

20

THE TEARS WERE really coming now, and one fat stripe rolled along the barrel of the gun and down the loop around the trigger to burst flat against my index finger. Raymond Hessel closed both eyes so I pressed the gun hard against his temple so he would always feel it pressing right there and I was beside him and this was his life and he could be dead at any moment.

This wasn't a cheap gun, and I wondered if salt might fuck it up.

Everything had gone so easy, I wondered. I'd done everything the mechanic said to do. This was why we needed to buy a gun. This was doing my homework.

We each had to bring Tyler twelve driver's licenses. This would prove we each made twelve human sacrifices.

I parked tonight, and I waited around the block for Raymond Hessel to finish his shift at the all-night Korner Mart, and around midnight he was waiting for a night owl bus when I finally walked up and said, hello.

Raymond Hessel, Raymond didn't say anything. Probably he figured I was after his money, his minimum wage, the fourteen dollars in his wallet. Oh, Raymond Hessel, all twenty-three years of you, when you started crying, tears rolling down the barrel of my gun pressed to your temple, no, this wasn't about money. Not everything is about money.

You didn't even say, hello.

You're not your sad little wallet.

I said, nice night, cold but clear.

You didn't even say, hello.

I said, don't run, or I'll have to shoot you in the back. I had the gun out, and I was wearing a latex glove so if the gun ever became a people's exhibit A, there'd be nothing on it except the dried tears of Raymond Hessel, Caucasian, aged twenty-three with no distinguishing marks.

Then I had your attention. Your eyes were big enough that even in the streetlight I could see they were antifreeze green.

You were jerking backward and backward a little more every time the gun touched your face, as if the barrel was too hot or too cold. Until I said, don't step back, and then you let the gun touch you, but even then you rolled your head up and away from the barrel.

You gave me your wallet like I asked.

Your name was Raymond K. Hessel on your driver's license. You live at 1320 SE Benning, apartment A. That had to be a basement apartment. They usually give basement apartments letters instead of numbers.

Raymond K. K. K. K. K. Hessel, I was talking to you.

Your head rolled up and away from the gun, and you said, yeah. You said, yes, you lived in a basement.

You had some pictures in the wallet, too. There was your mother.

This was a tough one for you, you'd have to open your eyes and see the picture of Mom and Dad smiling and see the gun at the same time, but you did, and then your eyes closed and you started to cry.

You were going to cool, the amazing miracle of death. One minute, you're a person, the next minute, you're an object, and Mom and Dad would have to call old doctor whoever and get your dental records because there wouldn't be much left of your face, and Mom and Dad, they'd always expected so much more from you and, no, life wasn't fair, and now it was come to this.

Fourteen dollars.

This, I said, is this your mom?

Yeah. You were crying, sniffing, crying. You swallowed. Yeah.

You had a library card. You had a video movie rental card. A social security card. Fourteen dollars cash. I wanted to take the bus pass, but the mechanic said to only take the driver's license. An expired community college student card.

You used to study something.

You'd worked up a pretty intense cry at this point so I pressed the gun a little harder against your cheek, and you started to step back until I said, don't move or you're dead right here. Now, what did you study?

Where?

In college, I said. You have a student card.

Oh, you didn't know, sob, swallow, sniff, stuff, biology.

Listen, now, you're going to die, Ray-mond K. K. K. Hessel, tonight. You might die in one second or in one hour, you decide. So lie to me. Tell me the first thing off the top of your head. Make something up. I don't give a shit. I have the gun.

Finally, you were listening and coming out of the little tragedy in your head.

Fill in the blank. What does Raymond Hessel want to be when he grows up?

Go home, you said you just wanted to go home, please.

No shit, I said. But after that, how did you want to spend your life? If you could do anything in the world.

Make something up.

You didn't know.

Then you're dead right now, I said. I said, now turn your head.

Death to commence in ten, in nine, in eight.

A vet, you said. You want to be a vet, a veterinarian.

That means animals. You have to go to school for that.

It means too much school, you said.

You could be in school working your ass off, Raymond Hessel, or you could be dead. You choose. I stuffed your wallet into the back pocket of your jeans. So you really wanted to be an animal doctor. I took the saltwater muzzle of the gun off one cheek and pressed it against the other. Is that what you've always wanted to be, Dr. Raymond K. K. K. K. Hessel, a veterinarian?

Yeah.

No shit?

No. No, you meant, yeah, no shit. Yeah.

Okay, I said, and I pressed the wet end of the muzzle to the tip of your chin, and then the tip of your nose, and everywhere I pressed the muzzle, it left a shining wet ring of your tears.

So, I said, go back to school. If you wake up tomorrow morning, you find a way to get back into school.

I pressed the wet end of the gun on each cheek, and then on your chin, and then against your forehead and left the muzzle pressed there. You might as well be dead right now, I said.

I have your license.

I know who you are. I know where you live. I'm keeping your license, and I'm going to check on you, mister Raymond K. Hessel. In three months, and then in six months, and then in a year, and if you aren't back in school on your way to being a veterinarian, you will be dead.

You didn't say anything.

Get out of here, and do your little life, but remember I'm watching you, Raymond Hessel, and I'd rather kill you than see you working a shit job for just enough money to buy cheese and watch television.

Now, I'm going to walk away so don't turn around.

This is what Tyler wants me to do.

These are Tyler's words coming out of my mouth.

I am Tyler's mouth.

I am Tyler's hands.

Everybody in Project Mayhem is part of Tyler Durden, and vice versa.

Raymond K. K. Hessel, your dinner is going to taste better than any meal you've ever eaten, and tomorrow will be the most beautiful day of your entire life.

21

YOU WAKE UP at Sky Harbor International.

Set your watch back two hours.

The shuttle takes me to downtown Phoenix and every bar I go into there are guys with stitches around the rim of an eye socket where a good slam packed their face meat against its sharp edge. There are guys with sideways noses, and these guys at the bar see me with the puckered hole in my cheek and we're an instant family.

Tyler hasn't been home for a while. I do my little job. I go airport to airport to look at the cars that people died in. The magic of travel. Tiny life. Tiny soaps. The tiny airline seats.

Everywhere I travel, I ask about Tyler.

In case I find him, the driver's licenses of my twelve human sacrifices are in my pocket.

Every bar I walk into, every fucking bar, I see beat-up guys. Every bar, they throw an arm around me and want to buy me a beer. It's like I already know which bars are the fight club bars.

I ask, have they seen a guy named Tyler Durden.

It's stupid to ask if they know about fight club.

The first rule is you don't talk about fight club.

But have they seen Tyler Durden?

They say, never heard of him, sir.

But you might find him in Chicago, sir.

It must be the hole in my cheek, everyone calls me sir.

And they wink.

You wake up at O'Hare and take the shuttle into Chicago.

Set your watch ahead an hour.

If you can wake up in a different place.

If you can wake up in a different time.

Why can't you wake up as a different person?

Every bar you go into, punched-out guys want to buy you a beer.

And no, sir, they've never met this Tyler Durden.

And they wink.

They've never heard the name before. Sir.

I ask about fight club. Is there a fight club around here, tonight? No, sir.

The second rule of fight club is you don't talk about fight club.

The punched-out guys at the bar shake their heads.

Never heard of it. Sir. But you might find this fight club of yours in Seattle, sir.

You wake up at Meigs Field and call Marla to see what's happening on Paper Street. Marla says now all the space monkeys are shaving their heads. Their electric razor gets hot and now the whole house smells like singed hair. The space monkeys are using lye to burn off their fingerprints.

You wake up at SeaTac.

Set your watch back two hours.

The shuttle takes you to downtown Seattle, and the first bar you go into, the bartender is wearing a neck brace that tilts his head back so far he has to look down his purple smashed eggplant of a nose to grin at you.

The bar is empty, and the bartender says, "Welcome back, sir."

I've never been to this bar, ever, ever before.

I ask if he knows the name Tyler Durden.

The bartender grins with his chin stuck out above the top of the white neck brace and asks, "Is this a test?"

Yeah, I say, it's a test. Has he ever met Tyler Durden?

"You stopped in last week, Mr. Durden," he says. "Don't you remember?"

Tyler was here.

"You were here, sir."

I've never been in here before tonight.

"If you say so, sir," the bartender says, "but Thursday night, you came in to ask how soon the police were planning to shut us down."

Last Thursday night, I was awake all night with the insomnia, wondering was I awake, was I sleeping. I woke up late Friday morning, bone tired and feeling I hadn't ever had my eyes closed.

"Yes, sir," the bartender says, "Thursday night, you were standing right where you are now and you were asking me about the police crackdown, and you were asking me how many guys we had to turn away from the Wednesday night fight club."

The bartender twists his shoulders and braced neck to look around the empty bar and says, "There's nobody that's going to hear, Mr. Durden, sir. We had a twenty-seven-count turn-away, last night. The place is always empty the night after fight club."

Every bar I've walked into this week, everybody's called me sir.

Every bar I go into, the beat-up fight club guys all start to look alike. How can a stranger know who I am?

"You have a birthmark, Mr. Durden," the bartender says. "On your foot. It's shaped like a dark red Australia with New Zealand next to it."

Only Marla knows this. Marla and my father. Not even Tyler knows this. When I go to the beach, I sit with that foot tucked under me.

The cancer I don't have is everywhere, now.

"Everybody in Project Mayhem knows, Mr. Durden." The bartender holds up his hand, the back of his hand toward me, a kiss burned into the back of his hand.

My kiss?

Tyler's kiss.

"Everybody knows about the birthmark," the bartender says. "It's part of the legend. You're turning into a fucking legend, man."

I call Marla from my Seattle motel room to ask if we've ever done it.

You know.

Long distance, Marla says, "What?"

Slept together.

"What!"

Have I ever, you know, had sex with her?

"Christ!"

Well?

"Well?" she says.

Have we ever had sex?

"You are such a piece of shit."

Have we had sex?

"I could kill you!"

Is that a yes or a no?

"I knew this would happen," Marla says. "You're such a flake. You love me. You ignore me. You save my life, then you cook my mother into soap."

I pinch myself.

I ask Marla how me met.

"In that testicle cancer thing," Marla says. "Then you saved my life."

I saved her life?

"You saved my life."

Tyler saved her life.

"You saved my life."

I stick my finger through the hole in my cheek and wiggle the finger around. This should be good for enough major league pain to wake me up.

Marla says, "You saved my life. The Regent Hotel. I'd accidentally attempted suicide. Remember?"

Oh.

"That night," Marla says, "I said I wanted to have your abortion."

We've just lost cabin pressure.

I ask Marla what my name is.

We're all going to die.

Marla says, "Tyler Durden. Your name is Tyler Butt-Wipe-for-Brains Durden. You live at 5123 NE Paper Street which is currently teeming with your little disciples shaving their heads and burning their skin off with lye."

I've got to get some sleep.

"You've got to get your ass back here," Marla yells over the phone, "before those little trolls make soap out of me."

I've got to find Tyler.

The scar on her hand, I ask Marla, how did she get it?

"You," Marla says. "You kissed my hand."

I've got to find Tyler.

I've got to get some sleep.

I've got to sleep.

I've got to go to sleep.

I tell Marla goodnight, and Marla's screaming is smaller, smaller, smaller, gone as I reach over and hang up the phone.

22

ALL NIGHT LONG, your thoughts are on the air.

Am I sleeping? Have I slept at all? This is the insomnia.

Try to relax a little more with every breath out, but your heart's still racing and your thoughts tornado in your head.

Nothing works. Not guided meditation.

You're in Ireland.

Not counting sheep.

You count up the days, hours, minutes since you can remember falling asleep. Your doctor laughed. Nobody ever died from lack of sleep. The old bruised fruit way your face looks, you'd think you were dead.

After three o'clock in the morning in a motel bed in Seattle, it's too late for you to find a cancer support group. Too late to find some little blue Amytal Sodium capsules or lipstick-red Seconals, the whole

Valley of the Dolls playset. After three in the morning, you can't get into a fight club.

You've got to find Tyler.

You've got to get some sleep.

Then you're awake, and Tyler's standing in the dark next to the bed. You wake up.

The moment you were falling asleep, Tyler was standing there saying, "Wake up. Wake up, we solved the problem with the police here in Seattle. Wake up."

The police commissioner wanted a crackdown on what he called gang-type activity and after-hours boxing clubs.

"But not to worry," Tyler says. "Mister police commissioner shouldn't be a problem," Tyler says. "We have him by the balls, now."

I ask if Tyler's been following me.

"Funny," Tyler says, "I wanted to ask you the same thing. You talked about me to other people, you little shit. You broke your promise."

Tyler was wondering when I'd figure him out.

"Every time you fall asleep," Tyler says, "I run off and do something wild, something crazy, something completely out of my mind."

Tyler kneels down next to the bed and whispers, "Last Thursday, you fell asleep, and I took a plane to Seattle for a little fight club look-see. To check the turn-away numbers, that sort of thing. Look for new talent. We have Project Mayhem in Seattle, too."

Tyler's fingertip traces the swelling along my eyebrows. "We have Project Mayhem in Los Angeles and Detroit, a big Project Mayhem going on in Washington, D.C., in New York. We have Project Mayhem in Chicago like you would not believe."

Tyler says, "I can't believe you broke your promise. The first rule is you don't talk about fight club."

He was in Seattle last week when a bartender in a neck brace told him that the police were going to crack down on fight clubs. The police commissioner himself wanted it special.

"What it is," Tyler says, "is we have police who come to fight at fight club and really like it. We have newspaper reporters and law clerks and lawyers, and we know everything before it's going to happen."

We were going to be shut down.

"At least in Seattle," Tyler says.

I ask what did Tyler do about it.

"What did *we* do about it," Tyler says.

We called an Assault Committee meeting.

"There isn't a me and a you, anymore," Tyler says, and he pinches the end of my nose. "I think you've figured that out."

We both use the same body, but at different times.

"We called a special homework assignment," Tyler says. "We said, 'Bring me the steaming testicles of his esteemed honor, Seattle Police Commissioner Whoever.' "

I'm not dreaming.

"Yes," Tyler says, "you are."

We put together a team of fourteen space monkeys, and five of these space monkeys were police, and we were every person in the park where his honor walks his dog, tonight.

"Don't worry," Tyler says, "the dog is alright."

The whole attack took three minutes less than our best run-through. We'd projected twelve minutes. Our best run-through was nine minutes.

We have five space monkeys hold him down.

Tyler's telling me this, but somehow, I already know it.

Three space monkeys were on lookout.

One space monkey did the ether.

One space monkey tugged down his esteemed sweatpants.

The dog is a spaniel, and it's just barking and barking.

Barking and barking.

Barking and barking.

One space monkey wrapped the rubber band three times until it was tight around the top of his esteemed sack.

"One monkey's between his legs with the knife," Tyler whispers with his punched-out face by my ear. "And I'm whispering in his most esteemed police commissioner's ear that he better stop the fight club crackdown, or we'll tell the world that his esteemed honor does not have any balls."

Tyler whispers, "How far do you think you'll get, your honor?"

The rubber band is cutting off any feeling down there.

"How far do you think you'll get in politics if the voters know you have no nuts?"

By now, his honor has lost all feeling.

Man, his nuts are ice cold.

If even one fight club has to close, we'll send his nuts east and west. One goes to the *New York Times* and one goes to the *Los Angeles Times*. One to each. Sort of press release style.

The space monkey took the ether rag off his mouth, and the commissioner said, don't.

And Tyler said, "We have nothing to lose except fight club."

The commissioner, he had everything.

All we were left was the shit and the trash of the world.

Tyler nodded to the space monkey with the knife between the commissioner's legs.

Tyler asked, "Imagine the rest of your life with your bag flapping empty."

The commissioner said, no.

And don't.

Stop.

Please.

Oh.

God.

Help.

Me.

Help.

No.

Me.

God.

Me.

Stop.

Them.

And the space monkey slips the knife in and only cuts off the rubber band.

Six minutes, total, and we were done.

"Remember this," Tyler said. "The people you're trying to step on, we're everyone you depend on. We're the people who do your laundry and cook your food and serve your dinner. We make your bed. We guard you while you're asleep. We drive the ambulances. We direct your call. We are cooks and taxi drivers and we know everything about you. We process your insurance claims and credit card charges. We control every part of your life.

"We are the middle children of history, raised by television to believe that someday we'll be millionaires and movie stars and rock stars, but we won't. And we're just learning this fact," Tyler said. "So don't fuck with us."

The space monkey had to press the ether down, hard on the commissioner sobbing and put him all the way out.

Another team dressed him and took him and his dog home. After that, the secret was up to him to keep. And, no, we didn't expect any more fight club crackdown.

His esteemed honor went home scared but intact.

"Every time we do these little homework assignments," Tyler says, "these fight club men with nothing to lose are a little more invested in Project Mayhem."

Tyler kneeling next to my bed says, "Close your eyes and give me your hand."

I close my eyes, and Tyler takes my hand. I feel Tyler's lips against the scar of his kiss.

"I said that if you talked about me behind my back, you'd never see me again," Tyler said. "We're not two separate men. Long story short, when you're awake, you have the control, and you can call yourself anything you want, but the second you fall asleep, I take over, and you become Tyler Durden."

But we fought, I say. The night we invented fight club.

"You weren't really fighting me," Tyler says. "You said so yourself. You were fighting everything you hate in your life."

But I can see you.

"You're asleep."

But you're renting a house. You held a job. Two jobs.

Tyler says, "Order your canceled checks from the bank. I rented the house in your name. I think you'll find the handwriting on the rent checks matches the notes you've been typing for me."

Tyler's been spending my money. It's no wonder I'm always overdrawn.

"And the jobs, well, why do you think you're so tired. Geez, it's not insomnia. As soon as you fall asleep, I take over and go to work or fight club or whatever. You're lucky I didn't get a job as a snake handler."

I say, but what about Marla?

"Marla loves you."

Marla loves you.

"Marla doesn't know the difference between you and me. You

gave her a fake name the night you met. You never gave your real name at a support group, you inauthentic shit. Since I saved her life, Marla thinks your name is Tyler Durden."

So, now that I know about Tyler, will he just disappear?

"No," Tyler says, still holding my hand, "I wouldn't be here in the first place if you didn't want me. I'll still live my life while you're asleep, but if you fuck with me, if you chain yourself to the bed at night or take big doses of sleeping pills, then we'll be enemies. And I'll get you for it."

Oh, this is bullshit. This is a dream. Tyler is a projection. He's a disassociative personality disorder. A psychogenic fugue state. Tyler Durden is my hallucination.

"Fuck that shit," Tyler says. "Maybe you're *my* schizophrenic hallucination."

I was here first.

Tyler says, "Yeah, yeah, yeah, well let's just see who's here last."

This isn't real. This is a dream, and I'll wake up.

"Then wake up."

And then the telephone's ringing, and Tyler's gone.

Sun is coming through the curtains.

It's my 7 A.M. wake-up call, and when I pick up the receiver, the line is dead.

23

FAST-FORWARD, I fly back home to Marla and the Paper Street Soap Company.

Everything is still falling apart.

At home, I'm too scared to look in the fridge. Picture dozens of little plastic sandwich bags labeled with cities like Las Vegas and Chicago and Milwaukee where Tyler had to make good his threats to protect chapters of fight club. Inside each bag would be a pair of messy tidbits, frozen solid.

In one corner of the kitchen, a space monkey squats on the cracked linoleum and studies himself in a hand mirror. "I am the all-singing, all-dancing crap of this world," the space monkey tells the mirror. "I am the toxic waste by-product of God's creation."

Other space monkeys move around in the garden, picking things, killing things.

With one hand on the freezer door, I take a big breath and try to center my enlightened spiritual entity.

> Raindrops on roses
> Happy Disney animals
> This makes my parts hurt

The freezer's open an inch when Marla peers over my shoulder and says, "What's for dinner?"

The space monkey looks at himself squatting in his hand mirror. "I am the shit and infectious human waste of creation."

Full circle.

About a month ago, I was afraid to let Marla look in the fridge. Now I'm afraid to look in the fridge myself.

Oh, God. Tyler.

Marla loves me. Marla doesn't know the difference.

"I'm glad you're back," Marla says. "We have to talk."

Oh, yeah, I say. We have to talk.

I can't bring myself to open the freezer.

I am Joe's Shrinking Groin.

I tell Marla, don't touch anything in this freezer. Don't even open it. If you ever find anything inside it, don't eat them or feed them to a cat or anything. The space monkey with the hand mirror is eyeing us so I tell Marla we have to leave. We need to be someplace else to have this talk.

Down the basement stairs, one space monkey is reading to the other space monkeys. "The three ways to make napalm:

"One, you can mix equal parts of gasoline and frozen orange juice concentrate," the space monkey in the basement reads. "Two, you can mix equal parts of gasoline and diet cola. Three, you can dissolve crumbled cat litter in gasoline until the mixture is thick."

Marla and I, we mass-transit from the Paper Street Soap Company to a window booth at the planet Denny's, the orange planet.

This was something Tyler talked about, how since England did all the exploration and built colonies and made maps, most of the places in geography have those secondhand sort of English names. The English got to name everything. Or almost everything.

Like, Ireland.

New London, Australia.

New London, India.

New London, Idaho.

New York, New York.

Fast-forward to the future.

This way, when deep-space exploitation ramps up, it will probably be the megatonic corporations that discover all the new planets and map them.

The IBM Stellar Sphere.

The Philip Morris Galaxy.

Planet Denny's.

Every planet will take on the corporate identity of whoever rapes it first.

Budweiser World.

Our waiter has a big goose egg on his forehead and stands ramrod straight, heels together. "Sir!" our waiter says. "Would you like to order now? Sir!" he says. "Anything you order is free of charge. Sir!"

You can imagine you smell urine in everybody's soup.

Two coffees, please.

Marla asks, "Why is he giving us free food?"

The waiter thinks I'm Tyler Durden, I say.

In that case, Marla orders fried clams and clam chowder and a fish basket and fried chicken and a baked potato with everything and a chocolate chiffon pie.

Through the pass-through window into the kitchen, three line cooks, one with stitches along his upper lip, are watching Marla and me and whispering with their three bruised heads together. I tell the waiter, give us clean food, please. Please, don't be doing any trash to the stuff we order.

"In that case, sir," our waiter says, "may I advise against the lady, here, eating the clam chowder."

Thank you. No clam chowder. Marla looks at me, and I tell her, trust me.

The waiter turns on his heel and marches our order back to the kitchen.

Through the kitchen pass-through window, the three line cooks give me the thumbs-up.

Marla says, "You get some nice perks, being Tyler Durden."

From now on, I tell Marla, she has to follow me everywhere at night, and write down everywhere I go. Who do I see. Do I castrate anyone important. That sort of detail.

I take out my wallet and show Marla my driver's license with my real name.

Not Tyler Durden.

"But everyone knows you're Tyler Durden," Marla says.

Everyone but me.

Nobody at work calls me Tyler Durden. My boss calls me by my real name.

My parents know who I really am.

"So why," Marla asks, "are you Tyler Durden to some people but not to everybody?"

The first time I met Tyler, I was asleep.

I was tired and crazy and rushed, and every time I boarded a plane, I wanted the plane to crash. I envied people dying of cancer. I hated my life. I was tired and bored with my job and my furniture, and I couldn't see any way to change things.

Only end them.

I felt trapped.

I was too complete.

I was too perfect.

I wanted a way out of my tiny life. Single-serving butter and cramped airline seat role in the world.

Swedish furniture.

Clever art.

I took a vacation. I fell asleep on the beach, and when I woke up there was Tyler Durden, naked and sweating, gritty with sand, his hair wet and stringy, hanging in his face.

Tyler was pulling driftwood logs out of the surf and dragging them up the beach.

What Tyler had created was the shadow of a giant hand, and Tyler was sitting in the palm of a perfection he'd made himself.

And a moment was the most you could ever expect from perfection.

Maybe I never really woke up on that beach.

Maybe all this started when I peed on the Blarney stone.

When I fall asleep, I don't really sleep.

At other tables in the Planet Denny's, I count one, two, three, four, five guys with black cheekbones or folded-down noses smiling at me.

"No," Marla says, "you don't sleep."

Tyler Durden is a separate personality I've created, and now he's threatening to take over my real life.

"Just like Tony Perkins' mother in *Psycho*," Marla says. "This is so cool. Everybody has their little quirks. One time, I dated a guy who couldn't get enough body piercings."

My point being, I say, I fall asleep and Tyler is running off with my body and punched-out face to commit some crime. The next morning, I wake up bone tired and beat up, and I'm sure I haven't slept at all.

The next night, I'd go to bed earlier.

That next night, Tyler would be in charge a little longer.

Every night that I go to bed earlier and earlier, Tyler will be in charge longer and longer.

"But you are Tyler," Marla says.

No.

No, I'm not.

I love everything about Tyler Durden, his courage and his smarts. His nerve. Tyler is funny and charming and forceful and independent, and men look up to him and expect him to change their world. Tyler is capable and free, and I am not.

I'm not Tyler Durden.

"But you are, Tyler," Marla says.

Tyler and I share the same body, and until now, I didn't know it. Whenever Tyler was having sex with Marla, I was asleep. Tyler was walking and talking while I thought I was asleep.

Everyone in fight club and Project Mayhem knew me as Tyler Durden.

And if I went to bed earlier every night and I slept later every morning, eventually I'd be gone altogether.

I'd just go to sleep and never wake up.

Marla says, "Just like the animals at the Animal Control place."

Valley of the Dogs. Where even if they don't kill you, if someone loves you enough to take you home, they still castrate you.

I would never wake up, and Tyler would take over.

The waiter brings the coffee and clicks his heels and leaves.

I smell my coffee. It smells like coffee.

"So," Marla says, "even if I did believe all this, what do you want from me?"

So Tyler can't take complete control, I need Marla to keep me awake. All the time.

Full circle.

The night Tyler saved her life, Marla asked him to keep her awake all night.

The second I fall asleep, Tyler takes over and something terrible will happen.

And if I do fall asleep, Marla has to keep track of Tyler. Where he goes. What he does. So maybe during the day, I can rush around and undo the damage.

24

HIS NAME IS Robert Paulson and he is forty-eight years old. His name is Robert Paulson, and Robert Paulson will be forty-eight years old, forever.

On a long enough time line, everyone's survival rate drops to zero. Big Bob.

The big cheesebread. The big moosie was on a regulation chill-and-drill homework assignment. This was how Tyler got into my condominium to blow it up with homemade dynamite. You take a spray canister of refrigerant, R-12 if you can still get it, what with the ozone hole and everything, or R-134a, and you spray it into the lock cylinder until the works are frozen.

On a chill-and-drill assignment, you spray the lock on a pay telephone or a parking meter or a newspaper box. Then you use a hammer and a cold chisel to shatter the frozen lock cylinder.

On a regulation drill-and-fill homework assignment, you drill the phone or the automatic bank teller machine, then you screw a lube fitting into the hole and use a grease gun to pump your target full of axle grease or vanilla pudding or plastic cement.

It's not that Project Mayhem needed to steal a handful of change. The Paper Street Soap Company was backlogged on filling orders. God help us when the holidays came around. Homework is to build your nerve. You need some cunning. Build your investment in Project Mayhem.

Instead of a cold chisel, you can use an electric drill on the frozen lock cylinder. This works just as well and it's more quiet.

It was a cordless electric drill that the police thought was a gun when they blew Big Bob away.

There was nothing to tie Big Bob to Project Mayhem or fight club or the soap.

In his pocket was a wallet photo of himself huge and naked at first glance in a posing strap at some contest. It's a stupid way to live, Bob said. You're blind from the stage lights, and deaf from the feedback rush of the sound system until the judge will order, extend your right quad, flex and hold.

Put your hands where we can see them.

Extend your left arm, flex the bicep and hold.

Freeze.

Drop the weapon.

This was better than real life.

On his hand was a scar from my kiss. From Tyler's kiss. Big Bob's sculpted hair had been shaved off and his fingerprints had been burned off with lye. And it was better to get hurt than get arrested, because if you were arrested, you were off Project Mayhem, no more homework assignments.

One minute, Robert Paulson was the warm center that the life of the world crowded around, and the next moment, Robert Paulson was an object. After the police shot, the amazing miracle of death.

In every fight club, tonight, the chapter leader walks around in the darkness outside the crowd of men who stare at each other across the empty center of every fight club basement, and this voice yells:

"His name is Robert Paulson."

And the crowd yells, "His name is Robert Paulson."

The leaders yell, "He is forty-eight years old."

And the crowd yells, "He is forty-eight years old."

He is forty-eight years old, and he was part of fight club.

He is forty-eight years old, and he was part of Project Mayhem.

Only in death will we have our own names since only in death are we no longer part of the effort. In death we become heroes.

And the crowds yell, "Robert Paulson."

And the crowds yell, "Robert Paulson."

And the crowds yell, "Robert Paulson."

I go to fight club tonight to shut it down. I stand in the one light at the center of the room, and the club cheers. To everyone here, I'm Tyler Durden. Smart. Forceful. Gutsy. I hold up my hands for silence, and I suggest, why don't we all just call it a night. Go home, tonight, and forget about fight club.

I think fight club has served its purpose, don't you?

Project Mayhem is canceled.

I hear there's a good football game on television . . .

One hundred men just stare at me.

A man is dead, I say. This game is over. It's not for fun anymore.

Then, from the darkness outside the crowd comes the anonymous voice of the chapter leader: "The first rule of fight club is you don't talk about fight club."

I yell, go home!

"The second rule of fight club is you don't talk about fight club."

Fight club is canceled! Project Mayhem is canceled.

"The third rule is only two guys to a fight."

I am Tyler Durden, I yell. And I'm ordering you to get out!

And no one's looking at me. The men just stare at each other across the center of the room.

The voice of the chapter leader goes slowly around the room. Two men to a fight. No shirts. No shoes.

The fight goes on and on and on as long as it has to.

Picture this happening in a hundred cities, in a half-dozen languages.

The rules end, and I'm still standing in the center of the light.

"Registered fight number one, take the floor," yells the voice out of the darkness. "Clear the center of the club."

I don't move.

"Clear the center of the club!"

I don't move.

The one light reflects out of the darkness in one hundred pairs of eyes, all of them focused on me, waiting. I try to see each man the way Tyler would see him. Choose the best fighters for training in Project Mayhem. Which ones would Tyler invite to work at the Paper Street Soap Company?

"Clear the center of the club!" This is established fight club procedure. After three requests from the chapter leader, I will be ejected from the club.

But I'm Tyler Durden. I invented fight club. Fight club is mine. I wrote those rules. None of you would be here if it wasn't for me. And I say it stops here!

"Prepare to evict the member in three, two, one."

The circle of men collapses in on top of me, and two hundred hands clamp around every inch of my arms and legs and I'm lifted spread-eagle toward the light.

Prepare to evacuate soul in five, in four, three, two, one.

And I'm passed overhead, hand to hand, crowd surfing toward the door. I'm floating. I'm flying.

I'm yelling, fight club is mine. Project Mayhem was my idea. You can't throw me out. I'm in control here. Go home.

The voice of the chapter leader yells, "Registered fight number one, please take the center of the floor. Now!"

I'm not leaving. I'm not giving up. I can beat this. I'm in control here.

"Evict fight club member, now!"

Evacuate soul, now.

And I fly slowly out the door and into the night with the stars overhead and the cold air, and I settle to the parking lot concrete. All the hands retreat, and a door shuts behind me, and a bolt snaps it locked. In a hundred cities, fight club goes on without me.

25

FOR YEARS NOW, I've wanted to fall asleep. The sort of slipping off, the giving up, the falling part of sleep. Now sleeping is the last thing I want to do. I'm with Marla in room 8G at the Regent Hotel. With all the old people and junkies shut up in their little rooms, here, somehow, my pacing desperation seems sort of normal and expected.

"Here," Marla says while she's sitting cross-legged on her bed and punching a half-dozen wake-up pills out of their plastic blister card. "I used to date a guy who had terrible nightmares. He hated to sleep, too."

What happened to the guy she was dating?

"Oh, he died. Heart attack. Overdose. Way too many amphetamines," Marla says. "He was only nineteen."

Thanks for sharing.

When we walked into the hotel, the guy at the lobby desk had half his hair torn out at the roots. His scalp raw and scabbed, he saluted me. The seniors watching television in the lobby all turned to see who I was when the guy at the desk called me sir.

"Good evening, sir."

Right now, I can imagine him calling some Project Mayhem headquarters and reporting my whereabouts. They'll have a wall map of the city and trace my movements with little pushpins. I feel tagged like a migrating goose on *Wild Kingdom*.

They're all spying on me, keeping tabs.

"You can take all six of these and not get sick to your stomach," Marla says, "but you have to take them by putting them up your butt."

Oh, this is pleasant.

Marla says, "I'm not making this up. We can get something stronger, later. Some real drugs like cross tops or black beauties or alligators."

I'm not putting these pills up my ass.

"Then only take two."

Where are we going to go?

"Bowling. It's open all night, and they won't let you sleep there."

Everywhere we go, I say, guys on the street think I'm Tyler Durden.

"Is that why the bus driver let us ride for free?"

Yeah. And that's why the two guys on the bus gave us their seats.

"So what's your point?"

I don't think it's enough to just hide out. We have to do something to get rid of Tyler.

"I dated a guy once who liked to wear my clothes," Marla says. "You know, dresses. Hats with veils. We could dress you up and sneak you around."

I'm not cross-dressing, and I'm not putting pills up my ass.

"It gets worse," Marla says. "I dated a guy, once, who wanted me to fake a lesbian scene with his blow-up doll."

I could imagine myself becoming one of Marla's stories.

I dated a guy once who was a split personality.

"I dated this other guy who used one of those penis enlargement systems."

I ask what time is it?

"Four A.M."

In another three hours, I have to be at work.

"Take your pills," Marla says. "You being Tyler Durden and all, they'll probably let us bowl for free. Hey, before we get rid of Tyler, can we go shopping? We could get a nice car. Some clothes. Some CDs. There is an upside to all this free stuff."

Marla.

"Okay, forget it."

26

THAT OLD SAYING, about how you always kill the thing you love, well, it works both ways.

And it does work both ways.

This morning I went to work and there were police barricades between the building and the parking lot with the police at the front doors, taking statements from the people I work with. Everybody milling around.

I didn't even get off the bus.

I am Joe's Cold Sweat.

From the bus, I can see the floor-to-ceiling windows on the third floor of my office building are blown out, and inside a fireman in a dirty yellow slicker is whacking at a burnt panel in the suspended ceiling. A smoldering desk inches out the broken window, pushed by two firemen, then the desk tilts and slides and falls the quick three stories to the sidewalk and lands with more of a feeling than a sound.

Breaks open and it's still smoking.

I am the Pit of Joe's Stomach.

It's my desk.

I know my boss is dead.

The three ways to make napalm. I knew Tyler was going to kill my boss. The second I smelled gasoline on my hands, when I said I wanted out of my job, I was giving him permission. Be my guest.

Kill my boss.

Oh, Tyler.

I know a computer blew up.

I know this because Tyler knows this.

I don't want to know this, but you use a jeweler's drill to drill a hole through the top of a computer monitor. All the space monkeys know this. I typed up Tyler's notes. This is a new version of the lightbulb bomb, where you drill a hole in a lightbulb and fill the bulb with gasoline. Plug the hole with wax or silicone, then screw the bulb into a socket and let someone walk into the room and throw the switch.

A computer tube can hold a lot more gasoline than a lightbulb.

A cathode ray tube, CRT, you either remove the plastic housing around the tube, this is easy enough, or you work through the vent panels in the top of the housing.

First you have to unplug the monitor from the power source and from the computer.

This would also work with a television.

Just understand, if there's a spark, even static electricity from the carpet, you're dead. Screaming, burned-alive dead.

A cathode ray tube can hold 300 volts of passive electrical storage, so use a hefty screwdriver across the main power supply capacitor, first. If you're dead at this point, you didn't use an insulated screwdriver.

There's a vacuum inside the cathode ray tube so the moment you drill through, the tube will suck air, sort of inhale a little whistle of it.

Ream the little hole with a larger bit, then a larger bit, until you can put the tip of a funnel into the hole. Then, fill the tube with your choice of explosive. Homemade napalm is good. Gasoline or gasoline mixed with frozen orange juice concentrate or cat litter.

A sort of fun explosive is potassium permanganate mixed with powdered sugar. The idea is to mix one ingredient that will burn very fast with a second ingredient that will supply enough oxygen for that burning. This burns so fast, it's an explosion.

Barium peroxide and zinc dust.

Ammonium nitrate and powdered aluminum.

The nouvelle cuisine of anarchy.

Barium nitrate in a sauce of sulfur and garnished with charcoal. That's your basic gunpowder.

Bon appétit.

Pack the computer monitor full of this, and when someone turns on the power, this is five or six pounds of gunpowder exploding in their face.

The problem is, I sort of liked my boss.

If you're male, and you're Christian and living in America, your father is your model for God. And sometimes you find your father in your career.

Except Tyler didn't like my boss.

The police would be looking for me. I was the last person out of the building last Friday night. I woke up at my desk with my breath condensed on the desktop and Tyler on the telephone, telling me, "Go outside. We have a car."

We have a Cadillac.

The gasoline was still on my hands.

The fight club mechanic asked, what will you wish you'd done before you died?

I wanted out of my job. I was giving Tyler permission. Be my guest. Kill my boss.

From my exploded office, I ride the bus to the gravel turnaround point at the end of the line. This is where the subdivisions peter out to vacant lots and plowed fields. The driver takes out a sack lunch and a thermos and watches me in his overhead mirror.

I'm trying to figure where I can go that the cops won't be looking for me. From the back of the bus, I can see maybe twenty people sitting between me and the driver. I count the backs of twenty heads.

Twenty shaved heads.

The driver twists around in his seat and calls to me in the back seat, "Mr. Durden, sir, I really admire what you're doing."

I've never seen him before.

"You have to forgive me for this," the driver says. "The committee says this is your own idea sir."

The shaved heads turn around one after another. Then one by one they stand. One's got a rag in his hand, and you can smell the ether. The closest one has a hunting knife. The one with the knife is the fight club mechanic.

"You're a brave man," the bus driver says, "to make yourself a homework assignment."

The mechanic tells the bus driver, "Shut up," and "The lookout doesn't say shit."

You know one of the space monkeys has a rubber band to wrap around your nuts. They fill up the front of the bus.

The mechanic says, "You know the drill, Mr. Durden. You said it yourself. You said, if anyone ever tries to shut down the club, even you, then we have to get him by the nuts."

Gonads.

Jewels.

Testes.

Huevos.

Picture the best part of yourself frozen in a sandwich bag at the Paper Street Soap Company.

"You know it's useless to fight us," the mechanic says.

The bus driver chews his sandwich and watches us in the overhead mirror.

A police siren wails, coming closer. A tractor rattles across a field in the distance. Birds. A window in the back of the bus is half open. Clouds. Weeds grow at the edge of the gravel turnaround. Bees or flies buzz around the weeds.

"We're just after a little collateral," the fight club mechanic says. "This isn't just a threat, this time, Mr. Durden. This time, we have to cut them."

The bus driver says, "It's cops."

The siren arrives somewhere at the front of the bus.

So what do I have to fight back with?

A police car pulls up to the bus, lights flashing blue and red through the bus windshield, and someone outside the bus is shouting, "Hold up in there."

And I'm saved.

Sort of.

I can tell the cops about Tyler. I'll tell them everything about fight club, and maybe I'll go to jail, and then Project Mayhem will be their problem to solve, and I won't be staring down a knife.

The cops come up the bus steps, the first cop saying, "You cut him yet?"

The second cop says, "Do it quick, there's a warrant out for his arrest."

Then he takes off his hat, and to me he says, "Nothing personal, Mr. Durden. It's a pleasure to finally meet you."

I say, you all are making a big mistake.

The mechanic says, "You told us you'd probably say that."

I'm not Tyler Durden.

"You told us you'd say that, too."

I'm changing the rules. You can still have fight club, but we're not going to castrate anyone, anymore.

"Yeah, yeah, yeah," the mechanic says. He's halfway down the aisle holding the knife out in front of him. "You said you would *definitely* say that."

Okay so I'm Tyler Durden. I am. I'm Tyler Durden, and I dictate the rules, and I say, put the knife down.

The mechanic calls back over his shoulder, "What's our best time to date for a cut-and-run?"

Somebody yells, "Four minutes."

The mechanic yells, "Is somebody timing this?"

Both cops have climbed up into the front of the bus now, and one looks at his watch and says, "Just a sec. Wait for the second hand to get up to the twelve."

The cop says, "Nine."

"Eight."

"Seven."

I dive for the open window.

My stomach hits the thin metal windowsill, and behind me, the fight club mechanic yells, "Mr. Durden! You're going to fuck up the time."

Hanging half out the window, I claw at the black rubber sidewall of the rear tire. I grab the wheelwell trim and pull. Someone grabs my feet and pulls. I'm yelling at the little tractor in the distance, "Hey." And "Hey." My face swelling hot and full of blood, I'm hanging upside down. I pull myself out a little. Hands around my ankles pull me back in. My tie flops in my face. My belt buckle catches on the windowsill. The bees and the flies and weeds are inches from in front of my face, and I'm yelling, "Hey!"

Hands are hooked in the back of my pants, tugging me in, hugging my pants and belt down over my ass.

Somebody inside the bus yells, "One minute!"

My shoes slip off my feet.

My belt buckle slips inside the windowsill.

The hands bring my legs together. The windowsill cuts hot from the sun into my stomach. My white shirt billows and drops down around my head and shoulders, my hands still gripping the wheelwell trim, me still yelling, "Hey!"

My legs are stretched out straight and together behind me. My pants slip down my legs and are gone. The sun shines warm on my ass.

Blood pounding in my head, my eyes bugging from the pressure, all I can see is the white shirt hanging around my face. The tractor rattles somewhere. The bees buzz. Somewhere. Everything is a million miles away. Somewhere a million miles behind me someone is yelling, "Two minutes!"

And a hand slips between my legs and gropes for me.

"Don't hurt him," someone says.

The hands around my ankles are a million miles away. Picture them at the end of a long, long road. Guided meditation.

Don't picture the windowsill as a dull hot knife slitting open your belly.

Don't picture a team of men tug-of-warring your legs apart.

A million miles away, a bah-zillion miles away, a rough warm hand wraps around the base of you and pulls you back, and something is holding you tight, tighter, tighter.

A rubber band.

You're in Ireland.

You're in fight club.

You're at work.

You're anywhere but here.

"Three minutes!"

Somebody far far away yells, "You know the speech Mr. Durden. Don't fuck with fight club."

The warm hand is cupped under you. The cold tip of the knife.
An arm wraps around your chest.
Therapeutic physical contact.
Hug time.
And the ether presses your nose and mouth, hard.
Then nothing, less than nothing. Oblivion.

27

THE EXPLODED SHELL of my burned-out condo is outer space black and devastated in the night above the little lights of the city. With the windows gone, a yellow ribbon of police crime scene tape twists and swings at the edge of the fifteen-story drop.

I wake up on the concrete subfloor. There was maple flooring once. There was art on the walls before the explosion. There was Swedish furniture. Before Tyler.

I'm dressed. I put my hand in my pocket and feel.

I'm whole.

Scared but intact.

Go to the edge of the floor, fifteen stories above the parking lot, and look at the city lights and the stars, and you're gone.

It's all so beyond us.

Up here, in the miles of night between the stars and the Earth, I feel just like one of those space animals.

Dogs.

Monkeys.

Men.

You just do your little job. Pull a lever. Push a button. You don't really understand any of it.

The world is going crazy. My boss is dead. My home is gone. My job is gone. And I'm responsible for it all.

There's nothing left.

I'm overdrawn at the bank.

Step over the edge.

The police tape flutters between me and oblivion.

Step over the edge.

What else is there?

Step over the edge.

There's Marla.

Jump over the edge.

There's Marla, and she's in the middle of everything and doesn't know it.

And she loves you.

She loves Tyler.

She doesn't know the difference.

Somebody has to tell her. Get out. Get out. Get out.

Save yourself.

You ride the elevator down to the lobby, and the doorman who never liked you, now he smiles at you with three teeth knocked out of his mouth and says, "Good evening, Mr. Durden. Can I get you a cab? Are you feeling alright? Do you want to use the phone?"

You call Marla at the Regent Hotel.

The clerk at the Regent says, "Right away, Mr. Durden."

Then Marla comes on the line.

The doorman is listening over your shoulder. The clerk at the Regent is probably listening. You say, Marla, we have to talk.

Marla says, "You can suck shit."

She might be in danger, you say. She deserves to know what's going on. She has to meet you. You have to talk.

"Where?"

She should go to the first place we ever met. Remember. Think back.

The white healing ball of light. The palace of seven doors.

"Got it," she says. "I can be there in twenty minutes."

Be there.

You hang up, and the doorman says, "I can get you a cab, Mr. Durden. Free of charge to anywhere you want."

The fight club boys are tracking you. No, you say, it's such a nice night, I think I'll walk.

It's Saturday night, bowel cancer night in the basement of First Methodist, and Marla is there when you arrive.

Marla Singer smoking her cigarette. Marla Singer rolling her eyes. Marla Singer with a black eye.

You sit on the shag carpet at opposite sides of the meditation circle and try to summon up your power animal while Marla glares at you with her black eye. You close your eyes and meditate to the palace of the seven doors, and you can still feel Marla's glare. You cradle your inner child.

Marla glares.

Then it's time to hug.

Open your eyes.

We should all choose a partner.

Marla crosses the room in three quick steps and slaps me hard across the face.

Share yourself completely.

"You fucking suck-ass piece of shit," Marla says.

Around us, everyone stands staring.

Then both of Marla's fists are beating me from every direction. "You killed someone," she's screaming. "I called the police and they should be here any minute."

I grab her wrists and say, maybe the police will come, but probably they won't.

Marla twists and says the police are speeding over here to hook me up to the electric chair and bake my eyes out or at least give me a lethal injection.

This will feel just like a bee sting.

An overdose shot of sodium phenobarbital, and then the big sleep. Valley of the Dogs style.

Marla says she saw me kill somebody today.

If she means my boss, I say, yeah, yeah, yeah, yeah, I know, the police know, everyone's looking for me to lethally inject me, already, but it was Tyler who killed my boss.

Tyler and I just happen to have the same fingerprints, but no one understands.

"You can suck shit," Marla says and pushes her punched-out black eye at me. "Just because you and your little disciples like getting beat up, you touch me ever again, and you're dead."

"I saw you shoot a man tonight," Marla says.

No, it was a bomb, I say, and it happened this morning. Tyler drilled a computer monitor and filled it with gasoline or black powder.

All the people with real bowel cancers are standing around watching this.

"No," Marla says. "I followed you to the Pressman Hotel, and you were a waiter at one of those murder mystery parties."

The murder mystery parties, rich people would come to the hotel for a big dinner party, and act out a sort of Agatha Christie story. Sometime between the Boudin of Gravlax and the Saddle of Venison, the lights would go out for a minute and someone would fake getting killed. It's supposed to be a fun let's-pretend sort of death.

The rest of the meal, the guests would get drunk and eat their Madeira Consommé and try to find clues to who among them was a psychotic killer.

Marla yells, "You shot the mayor's special envoy on recycling!"

Tyler shot the mayor's special envoy on whatever.

Marla says, "And you don't even have cancer!"

It happens that fast.

Snap your fingers.

Everyone's looking.

I yell, you don't have cancer either!

"He's been coming here for two years," Marla shouts, "and he doesn't have anything!"

I'm trying to save your life!

"What? Why does my life need saving?"

Because you've been following me. Because you followed me tonight, because you saw Tyler Durden kill someone, and Tyler will kill anybody who threatens Project Mayhem.

Everybody in the room looks snapped out of their little tragedies. Their little cancer thing. Even the people on pain meds look wide-eyed and alert.

I say to the crowd, I'm sorry. I never meant any harm. We should go. We should talk about this outside.

Everybody goes, "No! Stay! What else?"

I didn't kill anybody, I say. I'm not Tyler Durden. He's the other side of my split personality. I say, has anybody here seen the movie *Sybil?*

Marla says, "So who's going to kill me?"

Tyler.

"You?"

Tyler, I say, but I can take care of Tyler. You just have to watch out for the members of Project Mayhem. Tyler might've given them orders to follow you or kidnap you or something.

"Why should I believe any of this?"

It happens that fast.

I say, because I think I like you.

Marla says, "Not love?"

This is a cheesy enough moment, I say. Don't push it.

Everybody watching smiles.

I have to go. I have to get out of here. I say, watch out for guys with shaved heads or guys who look beat up. Black eyes. Missing teeth. That sort of thing.

And Marla says, "So where are you going?"

I have to take care of Tyler Durden.

28

HIS NAME WAS Patrick Madden, and he was the mayor's special envoy on recycling. His name was Patrick Madden, and he was an enemy of Project Mayhem.

I walk out into the night around First Methodist, and it's all coming back to me.

All the things that Tyler knows are all coming back to me.

Patrick Madden was compiling a list of bars where fight clubs met.

All of the sudden, I know how to run a movie projector. I know how to break locks and how Tyler had rented the house on Paper Street just before he revealed himself to me at the beach.

I know why Tyler had occurred. Tyler loved Marla. From the first night I met her, Tyler or some part of me had needed a way to be with Marla.

Not that any of this matters. Not now. But all the details are coming back to me as I walk through the night to the closest fight club.

There's a fight club in the basement of the Armory Bar on Saturday nights. You can probably find it on the list Patrick Madden was compiling, poor dead Patrick Madden.

Tonight, I go to the Armory Bar and the crowds part zipper style when I walk in. To everybody there, I am Tyler Durden the Great and Powerful. God and father.

All around me I hear, "Good evening, sir."

"Welcome to fight club, sir."

"Thank you for joining us, sir."

Me, my monster face just starting to heal. The hole in my face smiling through my cheek. A frown on my real mouth.

Because I'm Tyler Durden, and you can kiss my ass, I register to fight every guy in the club that night. Fifty fights. One fight at a time. No shoes. No shirts.

The fights go on as long as they have to.

And if Tyler loves Marla.

I love Marla.

And what happens doesn't happen in words. I want to smother all the French beaches I'll never see. Imagine stalking elk through the damp canyon forests around Rockefeller Center.

The first fight I get, the guy gets me in a full nelson and rams my face, rams my cheek, rams the hole in my cheek into the concrete floor until my teeth inside snap off and plant their jagged roots into my tongue.

Now I can remember Patrick Madden, dead on the floor, his little figurine of a wife, just a little girl with a chignon. His wife giggled and tried to pour champagne between her dead husband's lips.

The wife said the fake blood was too, too red. Mrs. Patrick Madden put two fingers in the blood pooled next to her husband and then put the fingers in her mouth.

The teeth planted in my tongue, I taste the blood.

Mrs. Patrick Madden tasted the blood.

I remember being there on the outskirts of the murder mystery party with the space monkey waiters standing bodyguard around me. Marla in her dress with a wallpaper pattern of dark roses watched from the other side of the ballroom.

My second fight, the guy puts a knee between my shoulder blades. The guy pulls both my arms together behind my back, and slams my chest into the concrete floor. My collarbone on one side, I hear it snap.

I would do the Elgin Marbles with a sledgehammer and wipe my ass with the *Mona Lisa.*

Mrs. Patrick Madden held her two bloody fingers up, the blood climbing the cracks between her teeth, and the blood ran down her fingers, down her wrist, across a diamond bracelet, and to her elbow where it dripped.

Fight number three, I wake up and it's time for fight number three. There are no more names in fight club.

You aren't your name.

You aren't your family.

Number three seems to know what I need and holds my head in the dark and the smother. There's a sleeper hold that gives you just enough air to stay awake. Number three holds my head in the crook of his arm, the way he'd hold a baby or a football, in the crook of his arm, and hammers my face with the pounding molar of his clenched fist.

Until my teeth bite through the inside of my cheek.

Until the hole in my cheek meets the corner of my mouth, the two run together into a ragged leer that opens from under my nose to under my ear.

Number three pounds until his fist is raw.

Until I'm crying.

How everything you ever love will reject you or die.

Everything you ever create will be thrown away.

Everything you're proud of will end up as trash.

I am Ozymandias, king of kings.

One more punch and my teeth click shut on my tongue. Half of my tongue drops to the floor and gets kicked away.

The little figurine of Mrs. Patrick Madden knelt on the floor next to the body of her husband, the rich people, the people they called friends, towering drunk around her and laughing.

The wife, she said, "Patrick?"

The pool of blood spreading wider and wider until it touches her skirt.

She says, "Patrick, that's enough, stop being dead."

The blood climbs the hem of her skirt, capillary action, thread to thread, climbing her skirt.

Around me the men of Project Mayhem are screaming.

Then Mrs. Patrick Madden is screaming.

And in the basement of the Armory Bar, Tyler Durden slips to the floor in a warm jumble. Tyler Durden the great, who was perfect for one moment, and who said that a moment is the most you could ever expect from perfection.

And the fight goes on and on because I want to be dead. Because only in death do we have names. Only in death are we no longer part of Project Mayhem.

29

TYLER'S STANDING THERE, perfectly handsome and an angel in his everything-blond way. My will to live amazes me.

Me, I'm a bloody tissue sample dried on a bare mattress in my room at the Paper Street Soap Company.

Everything in my room is gone.

My mirror with a picture of my foot from when I had cancer for ten minutes. Worse than cancer. The mirror is gone. The closet door is open and my six white shirts, black pants, underwear, socks, and shoes are gone.

Tyler says, "Get up."

Under and behind and inside everything I took for granted, something horrible has been growing.

Everything has fallen apart.

The space monkeys are cleared out. Everything is relocated, the liposuction fat, the bunk beds, the money, especially the money. Only the garden is left behind, and the rented house.

Tyler says, "The last thing we have to do is your martyrdom thing. Your big death thing."

Not like death as a sad, downer thing, this was going to be death as a cheery, empowering thing.

Oh, Tyler, I hurt. Just kill me here.

"Get up."

Kill me, already. Kill me. Kill me. Kill me. Kill me.

"It has to be big," Tyler says. "Picture this: you on top of the world's tallest building, the whole building taken over by Project Mayhem. Smoke rolling out the windows. Desks falling into the crowds on the street. A real opera of a death, that's what you're going to get."

I say, no. You've used me enough.

"If you don't cooperate, we'll go after Marla."

I say, lead the way.

"Now get the fuck out of bed," Tyler said, "and get your ass into the fucking car."

So Tyler and I are up on top of the Parker-Morris Building with the gun stuck in my mouth.

We're down to our last ten minutes.

The Parker-Morris Building won't be here in ten minutes. I know this because Tyler knows this.

The barrel of the gun pressed against the back of my throat, Tyler says, "We won't really die."

I tongue the gun barrel into my surviving cheek and say, Tyler, you're thinking of vampires.

We're down to our last eight minutes.

The gun is just in case the police helicopters get here sooner.

To God, this looks like one man alone, holding a gun in his own mouth, but it's Tyler holding the gun, and it's my life.

You take a 98-percent concentration of fuming nitric acid and add the acid to three times that amount of sulfuric acid.

You have nitroglycerin.

Seven minutes.

Mix the nitro with sawdust, and you have a nice plastic explosive. A lot of the space monkeys mix their nitro with cotton and add Epsom salts as a sulfate. This works, too. Some monkeys, they use paraffin mixed with nitro. Paraffin has never, ever worked for me.

Four minutes.

Tyler and me at the edge of the roof, the gun in my mouth, I'm wondering how clean this gun is.

Three minutes.

Then somebody yells.

"Wait," and it's Marla coming toward us across the roof.

Marla's coming toward me, just me because Tyler's gone. Poof. Tyler's my hallucination, not hers. Fast as a magic trick, Tyler's disappeared. And now I'm just one man holding a gun in my mouth.

"We followed you," Marla yells. "All the people from the support group. You don't have to do this. Put the gun down."

Behind Marla, all the bowel cancers, the brain parasites, the melanoma people, the tuberculosis people are walking, limping, wheel-chairing toward me.

They're saying, "Wait."

Their voices come to me on the cold wind, saying, "Stop."

And, "We can help you."

"Let us help you."

Across the sky comes the *whop, whop, whop* of police helicopters.

I yell, go. Get out of here. This building is going to explode.

Marla yells, "We know."

This is like a total epiphany moment for me.

I'm not killing myself, I yell. I'm killing Tyler.

I am Joe's Hard Drive.

I remember everything.

"It's not love or anything," Marla shouts, "but I think I like you, too."

One minute.

Marla likes Tyler.

"No, I like you," Marla shouts. "I know the difference."

And nothing.

Nothing explodes.

The barrel of the gun tucked in my surviving cheek, I say, Tyler, you mixed the nitro with paraffin, didn't you.

Paraffin never works.

I have to do this.

The police helicopters.

And I pull the trigger.

30

IN MY FATHER'S house are many mansions.

Of course, when I pulled the trigger, I died.

Liar.

And Tyler died.

With the police helicopters thundering toward us, and Marla and all the support group people who couldn't save themselves, with all of them trying to save me, I had to pull the trigger.

This was better than real life.

And your one perfect moment won't last forever.

Everything in heaven is white on white.

Faker.

Everything in heaven is quiet, rubber-soled shoes.

I can sleep in heaven.

People write to me in heaven and tell me I'm remembered. That I'm their hero. I'll get better.

The angels here are the Old Testament kind, legions and lieutenants, a heavenly host who works in shifts, days, swing. Graveyard. They bring you your meals on a tray with a paper cup of meds. The Valley of the Dolls playset.

I've met God across his long walnut desk with his diplomas hanging on the wall behind him, and God asks me, "Why?"

Why did I cause so much pain?

Didn't I realize that each of us is a sacred, unique snowflake of special unique specialness?

Can't I see how we're all manifestations of love?

I look at God behind his desk, taking notes on a pad, but God's got this all wrong.

We are not special.

We are not crap or trash, either.

We just are.

We just are, and what happens just happens.

And God says, "No, that's not right."

Yeah. Well. Whatever. You can't teach God anything.

God asks me what I remember.

I remember everything.

The bullet out of Tyler's gun, it tore out my other cheek to give me a jagged smile from ear to ear. Yeah, just like an angry Halloween pumpkin. Japanese demon. Dragon of Avarice.

Marla's still on Earth, and she writes to me. Someday, she says, they'll bring me back.

And if there were a telephone in Heaven, I would call Marla from Heaven and the moment she says, "Hello," I wouldn't hang up. I'd say, "Hi. What's happening? Tell me every little thing."

But I don't want to go back. Not yet.

Just because.

Because every once in a while, somebody brings me my lunch tray and my meds and he has a black eye or his forehead is swollen with stitches, and he says:

"We miss you Mr. Durden."

Or somebody with a broken nose pushes a mop past me and whispers:

"Everything's going according to the plan."

Whispers:

"We're going to break up civilization so we can make something better out of the world."

Whispers:

"We look forward to getting you back."